AMY MOVES IN

by MARILYN SACHS

Cover illustration by Ruth Sanderson

SCHOLASTIC BOOK SERVICES

New York Toronto London Auckland Sydney Tokyo

To Morris

The letter on pages 197 and 198 is from LAURA'S LUCK by Marilyn Sachs, © 1965 by Marilyn Sachs, and is reprinted by permission of Doubleday & Co., Inc.

ISBN 0-590-32301-6

This edition is published by Scholastic Book Services, a division of Scholastic Inc., 50 West 44 Street, New York, N.Y. 10036, by arrangement with Doubleday & Co., Inc.

12 11 10 9 8 7 6 5 4 3 2 1   9   1 2 3 4 5 6/8

Printed in the U. S. A.   01

Contents

The New Block   1

New Friends   16

The Family   32

School   46

The Park   62

Mama   82

Aunt Minnie and That Dog   98

More Pets   113

Rosa   125

April Fool   140

The Surprise Party   156

The Ball   174

Letters   191

The New Block

From where she stood on the stoop, Amy could hear the children's voices very clearly. They were jumping rope in front of the next house, and they chanted loudly:

> Down the Mississippi
> Where the boats go
> PUSH

> Down the Mississippi
> Where the boats go
> PUSH

She watched them hopefully. Perhaps one of them might come over in a moment and ask what her name was, or where she had lived before. From time to time she noticed some of the girls looking over at the moving van and then at herself. Should she smile at them, she wondered, or should she wait for them to smile first? What had they done on the old block when someone new moved in?

Two of the movers brought the sofa out from the van and rested it on the sidewalk. The sunshine played upon the faded flower design, and brought sharply into view the sagging bottom and all of the numerous scuff marks. "How old and ugly it looks," Amy thought. "Mama really should buy a new one." The sound of laughter made her turn her head. Two of the girls were looking at the sofa and giggling. As soon as they saw Amy watching them, they looked in another direction and pretended to be laughing at something else.

"What nasty girls!" Amy thought, her face turning red. "Nobody ever acted like that on the old block. Besides, what's so funny about an old sofa? I'm glad we don't have a new one." She remembered the way her friend Celia Gerber's mother had acted when she bought a new sofa. Nobody could even see what it looked like because it was always covered with old sheets and newspapers. Celia wasn't allowed to sit on it except when company came. Who wanted a sofa that you couldn't even sit on? Amy loved their sofa, and she certainly would never trade it in for a new one, and she was very glad when the movers carried it away, out of sight.

An empty feeling settled in Amy's stomach, and she wished she were home again, in the old neighborhood. At first, when Mama and Daddy had told her about moving, she had been excited and impatient to tell her friends. She and Celia had exchanged forget-me-nots. Right now the locket that Celia had given her encircled her neck, and when she moved her head she could feel it rubbing against her skin. She had promised Celia that she would wear the locket as long as she lived, and she *would*, even though her neck might turn green when the chain tarnished. She supposed Celia felt the same way about the diamond ring she had bought for her in the five-and-ten-cent store.

With all the excitement and fun involved in packing and moving, she had hardly thought about the new neighborhood. She had enjoyed helping Mama fold all the clothes and pack them in big cartons. Even more, she had enjoyed the many times they had to unpack everything because Laura's party shoes lay at the bottom of one of the boxes and she needed them for the school play, or because Daddy had left his fountain pen in the old blue jacket.

On the last night in the old apartment, no one in the family got to bed before midnight, Amy included. Mama kept saying wearily that they all should hurry up and finish their work and go to bed because the movers were coming very early, certainly no later than seven thirty in the morning.

When the movers finally did arrive the next day at one o'clock in the afternoon, the fun really started. Mama suddenly remembered some clothes hanging on the line; Daddy said his hat was missing; and Amy and Laura kept bumping into each other, the movers, Mama, and Daddy almost every time they turned around. But finally not a single carton or piece of furniture remained in the apartment.

It was then, while Amy walked through the empty rooms, taking a last look, that she suddenly began to feel that maybe she didn't really want to move after all. How strange the rooms looked without furniture! On the walls she saw patches of clean paint where the pictures had hung. Would the next people who moved in know that her baby picture had hung over the small patch in the back bedroom, or that the picture of "The Blue Boy" had covered the large patch in the living room? Mama came into the room and stood quietly for a moment, looking around her.

"Well, I suppose we had better go," she said softly. Amy held her hand as they walked down the stairs and looked up into Mama's tired face. She knew how much Mama hated to move.

Outside, the movers had stored all of their belongings in the van and called to them to hurry. She and Mama were going to ride with the movers, while Daddy and Laura took the trolley car. The prospect of a ride in the truck cheered Amy up again, but before stepping inside she took one last look at the block. Her eyes traveled over all of the familar sights that she had seen as long as she could remember, from the big yellow house at one corner to the candy store at the other. She knew it all so well. Even the cracks in the pavement were like old friends. She knew that the one in front of their house looked like a rabbit, while the one over at the corner curved like a graceful ballet dancer.

But now, here she stood on the new block where everything was so strange and unfamiliar. Her eyes moved past the girls jumping rope, and followed the row of houses all the way down the block. Were they really all exactly the same? How would she ever know which was hers? She looked up and down the block, but the last red brick house at one corner appeared to be just the same as the first red brick house at the other corner. How close the houses stood together! If one fell down, probably all of them would fall too.

She supposed a person could run across the rooftops from one end of the street to the other. She didn't have to mention it to Mama, but it would be nice trying it one day.

She glanced quickly across the street at the school and schoolyard that broke in between the houses. The closeness of the school had pleased Mama, but for Amy the small candy store that stood next to the yard presented a more attractive sight.

A woman came out of the house and looked curiously at Amy and then at the moving van. Did she live in their house? Amy wondered. Imagine not knowing your neighbors! Why, in the old house, she knew everybody and everybody knew her. She leaned her arm against one of the stone ledges that stood on either side of the stoop and watched the woman growing smaller and smaller as she walked away. The ledge felt hard and cold under her arm. She measured it with her eye and saw that it came just below her shoulder. "Pretty high," Amy thought, "but not too high!" A child who could climb a little would certainly have no trouble at all getting up on the top and dangling her feet high above the ground. If only her friend Celia were here, they could have so much fun on those ledges.

She glanced toward the girls again. They didn't look as nice as the girls on the old block, but she wished she knew them anyway. If one of them came over and asked her to play, she would even agree to be a steady ender and turn the rope for them constantly.

One of the girls was jumping now. Her feet leaped high over the rope, and her long straight hair flew up and down as she jumped. "That hair, that wonderful hair!" Amy thought sadly. The wind tossed her own hair against her face, and impatiently she shoved it away. She hated her hair. In all of her nine years Amy had wished for many things, but but there was only one wish that had never changed and, as far as she was concerned, never would. She wanted straight hair, real straight hair without a single wave in it, the kind of hair that became even straighter when it rained. Of course she wouldn't mind being taller, and she would gladly part with her bony knees, but if she could only have straight hair, nothing else would really matter. Sometimes when she lay in bed at night a beautiful story grew in her mind, and she almost believed that when she woke up the next morning she would find growing on her head long, absolutely black straight hair instead of her own blond frizzly curls. Things like that really never happened, she knew, except in fairy tales, but there was no harm in dreaming just a little bit, and in being just a little bit disappointed when the morning came.

Laura, her older sister who was eleven, had straight hair. Perhaps it was not exactly black, but it certainly was straight. Some people had all the luck! Whenever they were invited to a party or something special, Mama always put curlers in Laura's hair, and Laura could sleep in the curlers all night long. Laura generally complained about it, but for Amy nothing could be more thrilling. Once she asked Mama if she could sleep in curlers, and Mama laughed so hard that the tears rolled down her face. But when she saw Amy's unhappy face, she pinned a few curlers in her hair, and for one glorious afternoon Amy had worn them, and felt them bobbing up and down on her head. But when she took them off, that part of her hair looked just the same as the rest.

No one could really tell that Amy and Laura were sisters by looking at them. Laura was tall for her age, and chubby. Her hair was dark and so were her eyes. The only way people knew that they were sisters, Amy often thought sadly, was that she always had to wear the clothes that Laura had outgrown. Mama never seemed to realize that a big girl Amy's age had pride, and did not like dress pockets coming down below her hips, or

sleeves lapping over her fingers. She had discussed this with Mama many times, but
Mama always got back to the same old expla-
nation about not being able to afford it. She
said that she was sorry, "darling," but there
just wasn't enough money, and that Laura
outgrew clothes so quickly that they were
practically new anyway when Amy got them.

Sometimes it seemed to Amy that Mama
loved Laura better. Not all the time; certainly
not when Mama hugged her and called her
"mammela," or when she was sick and Mama
made all the things she liked to eat. But now,
for instance, Mama felt that when you moved,
someone had to keep an eye on the movers
to make sure they didn't "forget" to bring
in all the furniture, or that they weren't care-
less and broke something. Right now Mama
was busy inside unpacking the cartons. She
had asked Laura to go outside and watch
the movers, but Laura said, "Oh Mama, I'm
ashamed. I'm too old for that."

So Mama said, "All right. Amy, you go."

"If she's too old, I'm too old," Amy answered, but Mama just said, "Amy!" So here
she was, freezing in Laura's old winter coat
and keeping an eye on the movers. She felt
very embarrassed and silly, but she had to
admit that her presence did not seem to make
any impression on the movers. One of them

dropped a pillow into a puddle, and another one banged the leg of the green armchair up against the stoop so hard that Amy felt sure it must have broken. But no, the leg still remained fastened on. Should she say something to them? she wondered. After all, they were grownups. And besides, Mama hadn't told her to say anything, just to watch. So she continued to watch them. She pursed her lips together and wrinkled her forehead the way Mama did, hoping to give the movers the impression that she was wise and firm. But they hardly glanced at her.

Suddenly Amy heard a bark that seemed to come from below. She balanced herself on the ledge and looked down. There was a basement underneath the stoop and a flight of wooden stairs that led up to the level of the street. An iron gate with a locked iron door stood between the street and the stairs, discouraging any curiosity that might arise. She heard another bark, but still no dog appeared. Probably the superintendent lived down there, she reasoned, and the bark came from his dog.

"Here doggy, doggy, doggy," she cried.

How she loved dogs! But Mama never permitted them to have one. "An apartment house is no place," she always said. However, if a dog did live downstairs, it would be almost the same as having one in her own house. Certainly the super would allow her to play with the dog. He might even give her a key to the locked door so that she could go down there whenever she pleased. Amy could almost see the dog in her mind. He would be sort of a fox terrier, maybe all white with just a few black spots. Of course he would love her very much right away, and he would jump up on her whenever she played with him, and lick her face.

She would take him for walks, and then maybe one day she would get lost someplace. No one would be able to find her, and terror would spread through the neighborhood. But the dog would lead the way, and then Mama would hug him and say he was a fine dog. And then he would, no, *she* would have puppies, and Mama would...

Another bark interrupted Amy's thoughts, and up the stairs bounded the dog. One short look at him persuaded Amy that her plans might not work out so well after all. Never, in all her life, had she seen such a dog. Not only was he the largest dog she had ever set eyes upon, but the meanness of his face told Amy that this was a dog to keep away from. He had small glaring eyes, a flat ugly snout, and loose jowls. When he yawned, she could see long, sharp teeth. It was then that Amy became aware of the signs hanging on the gate, written on the stairs, and painted on the brick walls: BEWARE DOG, and KEEP OUT — DOG, and DOG.

The dog stretched out on the top step, but then, suddenly noticing Amy, he stood up again. Could he spring that great distance from the top of the stairs to the stoop? she wondered. She hardly thought he could, but she backed away just the same. A soft little whine escaped from the dog's throat and his tail began wagging merrily.

"If he thinks I'm going to pet him, he's crazy," Amy thought. "He probably just wants to get me over there so that he can bite me." She became so absorbed in watching the dog that she forgot all about the movers, and didn't notice another pillow falling into a puddle or the mattress dragging along the street.

While she stood wondering how big a bite he could take, she heard footsteps on the stairs. A man appeared, and as soon as she saw his face Amy realized that he must be the super. He and the dog looked very much alike. He was tall, and his face had the same kind of mean look that the dog's had. As soon as he reached the top step, the dog jumped up on him, but he pushed the dog and shouted,

"Get away from here, Buster. Lie down, you dumb dog."

The dog whined a little, but he lay down, his tail wagging again. "I wonder if the super is afraid to go to sleep at night," thought Amy. She felt his eyes upon her, and she turned away. Mama said it wasn't polite to stare at anyone, especially grownups.

"You one of the new kids?" the super finally asked.

"Yes," Amy answered politely.

"Don't let me catch you climbing on the stoop!"

"Oh no," said Amy quickly, "I never climb. I don't like to."

"That's fine," said the super, a little more pleasantly. "You and I'll get along fine. What's your name?"

"Amy Stern."

"I'm Mr. Williams, and this here's Buster."

"Does he bite?" Amy asked in a little voice.

Mr. Williams laughed. "Does he bite! Listen, this is the meanest dog in the whole country. I brought him up on raw meat, and he's not afraid of anything."

"Does he like children?" Amy said in a smaller voice.

"Hates them. Would tear them to pieces if I let him. You better keep away from him.

Once a boy climbed over the fence, and . . ." Mr. Williams shook his head sadly.

"What happened?" whispered Amy, her heart pounding. But she knew . . . That poor dead boy and that cruel, disgusting dog.

Mr. Williams just continued shaking his head. "And dogs," he finally said, "you should see what he does to dogs. Every single dog on this block crosses the street when they pass this house."

Amy's throat choked up suddenly. She felt that she had never hated anything or anybody in all her life as much as she hated that dog. Imagine, he had killed a boy and probably torn apart great numbers of small, helpless dogs. She hated to think of what he did to cats, but the vision of many bleeding, crying animals filled her mind, and she felt the tears coming to her eyes. Nobody had a dog like this in the old neighborhood. Only nice people and dogs lived there.

As Mr. Williams continued speaking happily about Buster's fierceness, a small white dog ambled up to the iron gate and stood looking at Buster. Buster rose to his feet, towering above the smaller dog. Only the gate separated them, but there was enough space between the bars for Buster to put through his ugly snout. Amy was just about to cry out in warning, when the little dog, in a quiet way, said, "Woof."

With a whine of great terror Buster turned and flew down the stairs like a flash of lightning. Mr. Williams ran after him, shouting, "You coward, you good-for-nothing coward! All you do is eat me out of house and home, and everything scares you. You good-for-nothing . . ."

As Amy turned to watch the girls jumping rope again, she felt happier than she had felt all day. Nobody looked in her direction, but now it hardly mattered. She would know them all very soon, maybe tomorrow, maybe the next day. But here was a whole new neighborhood for her to explore, new cracks in the pavement to discover, a tremendous schoolyard to throw balls in, all kinds of things to find out about. And perhaps, and she began to feel rather sure about this, there would be a dog to love and play with.

New Friends

Amy's eyes were scarcely opened the next morning when she remembered Buster. Laura still slept, her face buried in the pillow, but as Amy crawled over her to get out of the bed, she opened one sleepy eye, mumbled, "Where you going, dopey?" and promptly fell asleep again.

As she walked through the silent apartment, Amy saw with displeasure the scattered clothes waiting to be hung up, the unopened cartons, and all the other signs that promised a busy day for everybody. No sound came from her parents' bedroom, and she breathed happily. If she could only get outside before the family woke up, she wouldn't mind too much all the work in store for her. Today was Saturday, and that meant two glorious days remained before school started. She could certainly find out a good deal about the neighborhood between now and Monday. But first

16

of all, she wanted to see Buster again. She was quite sure that at this very moment he lay stretched out on the top step, as anxious as she to become acquainted. Quietly she managed to disentangle her corduroy slacks and a sweater from one of the cartons. How loudly that clock ticked! Mama was sure to wake up. She dressed quickly, slipped into her hat and coat, and walked carefully to the door. All remained silent. The door creaked a little as she opened it, and Amy stood waiting for Mama's voice. She heard only the ticking of the clock and the hissing of the radiator. Gently she closed the door behind her, and now safe, she ran noisily down the stairs and into the street.

Buster wasn't there. Even after she had pressed her face against the iron bars of the gate and hummed a little song, Buster still didn't appear. It was very disappointing. She had not supposed that Buster was the kind of dog who wasted his time sleeping.

Nobody else of importance was out yet either. Across the street, the schoolyard stretched out barren and forlorn. Amy's eyes moved up and down the block and came finally to rest on the candy store. At least that was open. It reminded her that she hadn't eaten her breakfast yet, and she was quite sure that a chocolate bar or a few Tootsie Rolls could pleasantly fill that empty spot in her stomach. Her hand rolled around inside her coat pocket until it felt a coin. She let her fingers slide around it, wondering whether it would turn out to be a nickel or a penny. Her allowance of twenty-five cents had certainly gone quickly this past week. She couldn't remember exactly how much remained, but she was inclined to believe that it would be a nickel. Gently her fingers rubbed against the surface of the coin. No question about it! Should she buy a few Tootsie Rolls with her nickel, she wondered, or should she spend it all on a chocolate bar? Lovingly she drew the coin from her pocket. It *was* a nickel!

She crossed the street and entered the store. Such a nice store, she decided immediately — not as large as the one in the old neighborhood, but there seemed to be plenty of interesting things. Amy walked over to the candy counter and examined its contents, one hand clutching the nickel in her pocket. On top of the counter stood a colorful display of cardboard boxes containing chocolates, nuts, and other delicacies, with the prices clearly marked on the outside of the boxes. Amy glanced quickly at these, but they held no real interest for her. Lower down, however, separated from her by a pane of glass, were arranged different varieties of candies, all colors and all shapes, but without any prices written on them. Amy stooped down and pressed her face against the glass, surveying carefully the three delightful rows that held the candies.

"Yes?" said Mr. Rosen pleasantly. "What can I do for you?"

Amy had been so occupied with examining the candy that she had forgotten all about the candy-store man. Reluctantly she pulled her eyes away from the counter and looked up at him. She saw a small, slender man with smooth white cheeks and a completely bald head.

"My," she thought, "he looks like a vanilla ice-cream cone." But she kept her thoughts to herself, smiled sweetly at him, and asked, "How much for those licorice sticks over there?" She pointed to a box down in one corner of the bottom row.

"Two cents."

Amy appeared thoughtful.

"Do you want that?" asked Mr. Rosen.

"No-o-o-o . . . how much for these jelly beans over here?" replied Amy, pointing to the next box.

"Two for a penny."

"And how much for these chocolate marshmallows?"

"Two cents."

"And how much for these gum drops?"

"Three for a nickel."

Amy continued asking questions, trying hard not to miss anything. Sometimes she felt it was more fun buying the candy than eating it. As long as you still held your money in your hand, you could wonder as long as you liked about whether you should buy one type of candy or another, and how much it cost, and what it would taste like. But once your money was gone and the candy eaten, why there was nothing else to look forward to.

"How much for those pink things?" Amy continued happily. By this time she had finished asking the prices of all the candies on the bottom row, and was now halfway through the middle row.

"Two cents," shouted Mr. Rosen. Amy looked up at him in surprise. He no longer looked so much like a vanilla ice-cream cone, because his face seemed to have become quite red.

"And how much . . ." Amy began again, but Mr. Rosen stopped her.

"Now listen," he said in a loud voice, "I haven't got time to stand here all day. Make up your mind."

"He's just like Mr. Murphy in the old store," Amy thought in surprise. "All right," she said brightly, "do you have any pretzels?"

"Of course I have pretzels," growled Mr. Rosen.

"I'll have a pretzel," Amy smiled.

Mr. Rosen hurried over to a large tin box at the other end of the store. The top seemed to be stuck, because, although he pulled and tugged at it, he couldn't open it. Finally he smacked it.

"Ouch," roared Mr. Rosen, holding his hand and standing on one foot. The hand grew very red.

"Is it broken?" Amy asked sympathetically, but Mr. Rosen didn't even answer her. He pulled again at the top, and this time it opened.

"Here, here," shouted Mr. Rosen, "here's your pretzel."

Amy shook her head, and smiled at him. "I don't want a round pretzel," she said softly. "I want a long pretzel."

Mr. Rosen certainly was a very foolish man, Amy decided. After she had spoken he just threw the pretzel back into the box, and she was sure it had broken. That was no way to treat pretzels, because who would want to buy a broken pretzel?

"Kids, kids, kids," roared Mr. Rosen as he tore open another box and practically threw a long pretzel at her. In a very ladylike manner Amy thanked him politely, handed him the nickel, and strolled out of the store. "What a strange man," she thought.

She began licking the salt on the pretzel. Amy had her own special way of eating pretzels. First she licked them for a while, until she couldn't stand the suspense any longer. Then she took a little bite from one end of the pretzel, and then a little bite from the other end. After that she took a few very little bites around the middle, and then finished it any way she liked. Every time she ate a pretzel, she tried to finish it in a different way. Crossing the street again, she licked away happily.

When she reached her house, there lay Buster on the top step. She stood a few feet from the iron gate, watching him. Nothing happened. She took a little step closer, but still nothing happened. Then she took a giant step, which brought her right up to the gate. Buster stood up. She took a giant step back. His tail began wagging.

"Nice doggie," she said, "nice doggie."

Buster seemed to be one big wagging tail. She took a giant step forward and Buster began a little, low whining in his throat. He stuck his snout out as far as it could go between the bars of the gate, and his red tongue lapped out at her. He certainly was irresistible, but he was also awfully big, and she could hardly help seeing his teeth behind his tongue. She just did not have the courage to put out a hand and touch that eager snout.

But before she knew what she was doing, her hand went out to him — the hand that held the pretzel. Buster happily licked the pretzel, and then stopped in great surprise. Evidently he had never tasted a pretzel before, and it was not likely that a dog who had been brought up on raw meat would take to this strange and different kind of food. However, Buster seemed determined to make friends, and not insult her by refusing what she had offered. Hesitantly he licked the pretzel again. This time he must have liked what he licked, because he took a bite, and then another, and then another. All the time Amy's hand came closer and closer to him, and then there was no pretzel left. She closed her eyes, but her hand remained outstretched. Only a second passed, but it was a long one, and then suddenly she felt what she had been longing to feel: a rough tongue licking her hand. They were friends!

By the end of the day Amy had made another friend, although this second friendship didn't start out as pleasantly as the first.

The family had been busy most of the day unpacking and putting everything in the right place. After Amy had helped Mama hang up the white lace curtains in the living room, Mama sighed a little bit and said, "I think you've done enough today, Amy. Why don't you go outside and play."

"Well, if you really don't need me," Amy replied, hustling into her coat and hat, and waiting only long enough to see Mama's tired smile.

She hurried outside. What a difference between now and this morning! Something important was happening everywhere she looked. In front of the next house a rope game was going on, the schoolyard seemed crammed full with children, and the sound of roller skates on sidewalk pavements rose to her ears. Should she walk over to the girls who were jumping rope? she wondered. Maybe if she stood there watching them, somebody might ask her to play. Or maybe she should go into the schoolyard. Well, she would think about it.

In the meantime she looked around her carefully. Neither Buster nor Mr. Williams, the super, was in sight. Quietly she climbed up onto the stone ledge and dangled her feet over the side. It was just grand sitting up there like a queen with all her subjects around her. Queen Amy, that's who she was, stolen at birth from the palace by jealous relatives. Her real mother and father were a king and queen, and Mama and Daddy were just good people who had taken her in, and whom she would reward in time. Her favorite daydream filled her mind, and she thought about all the money and jewels and castles that she would present to her friends.

Queen Amy had not been seated long on her throne when a ball smacked her on the head and dropped into her lap. It hurt, and for a moment everything seemed lost in the pain. Tears came to her eyes, and she put up her hand to feel her head.

"Hey, kid," someone called, "throw the ball here!"

Amy shook her head back and forth, and tried to collect her thoughts.

"Hey, kid," yelled the voice louder, "here!"

Amy looked in the direction of the voice. Across the street, in front of the schoolyard, stood a girl about Amy's age. She wore dungarees, a pair of sneakers, a big blue sweater, and her short red hair tumbled all around her face.

Amy's temper began to rise. Of all the nerve! Here this silly-looking tomboy hits her with a ball, doesn't even ask how she is or anything, and expects her to give back the ball without saying anything. Well, she would show her.

"Say, don't you understand English?" shouted the girl, crossing the street. "Come on, give me the ball!"

"You're the worst girl I ever met," Amy said, glaring at her. "Your ball hit me so hard on the head that I thought it was broken. I won't give you the ball until you apologize."

"You better give me the ball," answered the girl, coming up close to her, "or I'll give *you* something."

The girls in front of the next house stopped jumping rope and looked toward them. Amy could hear them whispering. She noticed that the girl was taller than she, and stronger too, she knew. What should she do? She became frightened, but her head still hurt, and her temper flared up again.

"All right," she said, "I'll give you the ball." She raised her hand above her head and threw the ball with all her might down the block. The ball rolled on, gathering speed as it went.

"Go and get it," she said nervously.

The girl squinted her eyes at Amy. "Now I'll give *you* something," she said, and she smacked Amy across the face, and then went flying down the block after the ball.

Amy began to cry. She always cried when someone hit her, not because it hurt so much but because she knew that she would be too

26

frightened to hit back. Amy never fought. She always ran to Mama, and Mama kissed her and hugged her, and told her at the same time that she had to learn to fight back if someone hit her first. Mama also hated fights and loud voices, but she believed that if you were right you should be able to defend yourself.

Although Amy agreed with Mama, she never could manage to fight back. And besides, she had Laura. Now Laura sometimes hit Amy, and seemed to enjoy it when she did. But there was one thing that Laura never could stand, and that was someone else hitting Amy. Whenever that happened, Laura went out, found the guilty one, introduced herself, and convinced the person that it would be healthier to leave Amy alone. After a while no one would hit Amy anymore. But this was a new neighborhood.

Amy ran into the house, crying so hard that she could hardly see where she was going.

"What is it, darling? What's the matter, sweetheart?" Mama cried in a frightened voice, and she picked Amy up into her lap and hugged her. Then she saw the red slap mark on Amy's face. Laura saw it too, and rushed into her coat.

"Where are you going?" said Mama sadly, because she knew where Laura was going.

"You know," said Laura. "Come on, Amy,

stop sniveling and just point her out to me."
Mama sighed.

Amy and Laura ran out into the street. The
girl was coming up the block, not running
anymore, just walking slowly and carrying
the ball in her hand.

"That's her," said Amy, climbing up onto
the stone ledge to watch.

Gracefully Laura walked over to the girl.
Quickly her hand darted out and grabbed the
other's sweater. The girl looked up at Laura
in surprise.

"Do you see that girl sitting on the stoop
there?" asked Laura quietly, as the girl struggled to free herself. "Well, that's my sister,"
Laura continued, smacking the girl. The girl
tried to hit Laura back, but Laura quickly
grabbed her arms. From long experience
fighting Amy's battles, Laura had become a
skillful fighter, although she scarcely ever became involved in a fight for herself.

"Well, that's my sister," Laura said again,
"and I don't want anyone to lay a hand on
her." She smacked the girl again. "Because if
anyone does, I'll fix her." And she shook the
girl from side to side. "Just remember that."
She gave the girl a final shake and then
shoved her away. Slowly Laura began walking back to the house without looking behind
her, to show her opponent that she had no fear

of a surprise attack. At first none seemed to be coming, because the girl looked tearful and frightened. But just before Laura reached the stoop, a woman came running out from the next house, grabbed Laura, and began shaking her.

"I saw the whole thing from the window," shouted the woman. "Shame on you, you big bully, hitting my daughter."

"Uh, uh, trouble," thought Amy, and she jumped off the ledge, ran into the house, and yelled, "Mama, Mama, they're hurting Laura!"

Mama didn't stop to ask questions. She snatched her coat and dashed out of the house.

The woman was still shaking Laura and shouting, "I don't care what Cynthia did, you're bigger than she is."

Mama ran right over and pulled Laura away. "How dare you lay a hand on my child?" asked Mama in a loud voice, glaring at the woman. It was so seldom that Mama raised her voice that Amy was surprised. Poor Mama, how she hated fights.

"How dare she lay a hand on my Cynthia?" answered the woman.

"If your daughter hadn't started the whole thing there wouldn't have been any trouble," Mama replied.

"Oh, is that so!" said the woman. "Well, you should teach your little girl to fight her own battles and not send your big bully out to fight them for her."

"My daughters," said Mama, "weren't raised to fight like common hoodlums. They're being raised to behave like ladies, which is more than I can say for your child."

Unfortunately Laura didn't look much like a lady, but Amy tried hard to assume an expression of dignity and good breeding. By this time a whole crowd of people had gathered around. Half of the schoolyard had emptied out, and other children were still running up from all directions. Windows were thrown open, and some of the more curious grownups had also joined the group, some listening, others smiling, and some trying to join in the conversation.

Cynthia began bouncing her ball up and down. The red marks on her face were disappearing. She looked at Amy, and Amy looked at her. She bounced her ball again. Then she looked at Amy again. This time she smiled, and Amy looked away shyly.

"You're new here, aren't you?" Cynthia asked.

Amy nodded. The ball bounced up and down a few times. Amy watched it and then looked at Cynthia. They smiled at each other.

"Want to play ball?" Cynthia asked softly.

"All right," said Amy very softly. And together they walked off, bouncing the ball between them, as Cynthia's mother said to Mama, "Well, let me tell you a thing or two...."

The Family

Sometimes when Amy thought about her mother, she felt ashamed. Of course Mama loved her, but there were times, Amy knew, when Mama was not proud of her. Mama always read the articles in ladies' magazines about bringing up children, and sometimes she brought home books from the library dealing with the same subject. Those books always made Amy uncomfortable, because she knew that the kind of children mentioned in the books as the right kind of children for parents to have were nothing like herself.

Mama would look strangely at her from time to time as she read those books, and she would even act differently. She would be very gentle with Amy, say nice things to her, and ask a lot of funny questions. But Amy didn't think the books helped Mama much, because sooner or later she would stop being so gentle and would tell Amy very firmly that there were certain habits Amy had which Mama did not appreciate at all.

For instance, Mama didn't care for the kind of friends Amy made. That Amy had made friends with Cynthia after involving the whole family except Daddy in the fight seemed downright disloyal to Mama. But even more than that, she said that Amy always made friends with the wrong kind of girls, the kind that liked to fight. Mama could not understand why this should be so.

"You're always getting into trouble," she said to Amy, "because you don't know how to pick your friends. You don't like to fight, and if someone hits you, you come crying into the house and Laura has to go out and fight your battles. It's not fair to Laura. Why don't you make friends with girls who also don't enjoy fighting? I'm sure there are many girls like that, although," and Mama sighed, "you never seem to find any."

Sometimes Mama invited a girl over to the house to meet Amy. Mama's face just beamed as she said, "This is Mrs. Kelly's granddaughter, Edith," or, "This is Mrs. Schwartz's daughter, Roslyn. She lives right around the corner."

It always turned out the same way. The girl would be neatly dressed, good in school, and polite to grownups. They would spend an afternoon playing casino or checkers if it were a rainy day, or if it were sunny, they would go outside with a ball and play "My Name Is" or some other bouncing game.

After the girl went home Mama would say, "Well, wasn't she a lovely girl? You really had a good time with her, didn't you?"

And Amy would answer, "She's O.K."

Mama's unhappy face made her feel sad. She was sorry that she had to hurt Mama's feelings, but she just couldn't work up any interest in girls like that. She wanted an exciting friend, like Cynthia, who could do all the things that she never dared to do. Nothing frightened Cynthia, grownups included. Cynthia could climb and run and fight as well as any boy, and the way she answered grownups back both astonished and delighted Amy. This was the kind of friend she wanted, someone whom she could admire with all her heart. She was proud and grateful that such a girl was willing to have her as a friend.

Besides this business about friends, there was something else about Amy that Mama worried about. Daddy always said that Amy had imagination, but Mama said that she told lies.

"You just don't understand me," Amy told Mama.

She really didn't tell lies, Amy thought; it was just that she liked making people happy. Somehow, when you made a person happy, something wonderful happened to you too.

For instance, Mama had a friend named Mrs. Greenberg. She was fat, and she had small eyes and a pasty face. Sometimes when she came to visit Mama, and Amy saw them sitting toether, she felt sad just looking at the difference between the two of them. Mama's pretty face, her soft brown hair and eyes, so close to the other woman's face, made Mrs. Greenberg seem even more homely. Amy felt she just had to do something to make up for Mrs. Greenberg's ugliness. So every time she came to visit, Amy managed to tell her how nice she looked or how pretty her dress was. One day when Mama had gone into the kitchen to make tea, Amy said to Mrs. Greenberg, "When I grow up, I hope I look just like you."

Actually Mrs. Greenberg was the last person in the world Amy wanted to look like. But when she saw how surprised Mrs. Greenberg looked, and then how happy, she was glad that she had said it. After that, very often when Mrs. Greenberg came to visit, she brought along a little present for Amy, or gave her some money for candy when no one was looking.

Amy found that most grownups, whether they were teachers, relatives, or friends, were like Mrs. Greenberg that way. They enjoyed hearing nice things about themselves, and Amy never minded telling them nice things. It made them very happy, and usually it made them like her very much. What could be wrong with that? She just could not understand why Mama should be at all disturbed.

Mama didn't see it that way, though, and just last week she had become very angry with Amy. The family had gone to visit Grandma and Grandpa, and while they were there, Grandma made some matzoh-brei[1] for everybody. Grandma made matzoh-brei differently from Mama. She took a whole piece of matzoh, soaked it in hot water, dipped it into egg, fried it, and served it with sugar. Mama, on the other hand, broke up the matzoh into little pieces, fried it like scrambled eggs, and served it with salt. After Amy had finished Grandma's matzoh-brei, she said, "Grandma, you make the best matzoh-brei in the whole world."

Grandma liked people to compliment her cooking, and she smiled at Amy and stroked her hair.

---

[1] Matzoh-brei: matzohs, or crackerlike, unleavened bread, fried with eggs.

But a few days later Mama made matzoh-brei, and when Amy finished eating she said, "Mama, nobody makes matzoh-brei as good as yours."

Mama wasn't pleased. She looked at Amy in an angry way, and then said, "Amy, you told Grandma just a few days ago that you like hers the best. It doesn't matter whose you like, but I don't want you to tell lies."

Amy felt cornered. She had forgotten all about Grandma's matzoh-brei, and now Mama kept looking at her, waiting for an answer. She began to feel sorry for herself, especially since she didn't particularly care for matzoh-brei anyway. It was awful the way Mama looked at her.

"I really like yours the best," she finally said, "but I wanted Grandma to be happy, so that's why I said it."

Mama sat down next to her. Her face wasn't angry any more, but she looked very serious.

"You know, Amy," she said, "it's a wonderful thing to want people to be happy. I think you have a very kind heart, and it makes me very pleased to know that."

Amy jumped up and wanted to hug Mama, but Mama stopped her and kept on talking.

"But when you lie to someone it doesn't really make them happy for long. Sooner or later they find out that you were lying, and it makes them feel sad because then they know you were making fun of them. And sooner or later you hurt yourself because, before you know it, you start lying about all kinds of things. And then you become all wrapped up in your lies and you can't get out.

Amy could almost see herself tied up in heavy ropes that became tighter and tighter the more she struggled. It was frightening, and she began to cry.

"I won't do it any more," she sobbed, and then she said, "Just don't hate me anymore."

Mama began to laugh. She pulled Amy into her lap and kissed her nose. "As if I could hate my baby," she said softly.

Mama was so wonderful, and Amy loved her so much. She loved Daddy too, but it was different with him. He didn't seem much interested in how Amy and Laura did in school, or in looking at their paintings and things like that. He just felt that his daughters were perfect, and no one had to prove it to him. Sometimes Amy overheard Mama talking to him about one of them, telling him something that worried her. But he seldom became upset. Once she heard Mama telling him how serious Amy's lying had become. Daddy just laughed and said he thought Amy was funny.

"She's got imagination, that's all," he said.

But when Mama kept insisting how serious it was, he said, "Hannah, of course it's not right to lie, but every now and then a little white lie doesn't hurt. Now your friend Mrs. Greenberg, for instance. The poor thing has probably gone through life without anyone ever telling her that she was pretty. Just think how much pleasure Amy gives her with those funny little white lies of hers. I think she comes here to see Amy, and not you anymore."

Daddy liked having good times. He enjoyed taking Amy and Laura out, and buying them sodas and putting them on the rides at Coney Island. He never forgot birthdays or anniversaries, and whenever he could he bought flowers for Mama.

"Oh, Harry," Mama usually said, angry and pleased at the same time, "we can't afford this. Sometimes I think I have three children instead of two." But she never could stay angry long at Daddy, although she always said sadly that money burned a hole in his pocket.

It always surprised Amy that the fathers of practically all her friends seemed to have one job that they had been working at for years. One might be a tailor, another a teacher or a bus driver, and so on. Daddy, however, never worked at one job for very long. He always found new jobs, and would come home, his eyes sparkling, anxious to tell about the exciting new kind of work he would be doing. Once he had been the manager of an office, another time he had gone into the printing business, and right now he sold insurance. Amy loved listening to Daddy's stories about all the different things he had done. However, she knew that Mama was never pleased when Daddy changed jobs.

"Not again, Harry!" Mama generally said.

Then Daddy would laugh and say she shouldn't worry, because he was sure that this was the right job for him. But it never really turned out that way. Sometimes Amy felt it was like a treasure hunt. You went from clue to clue until you finally found the treasure, and Daddy went from job to job, and someday, Amy knew, he would find the right one.

On Sunday Uncle Sam came to visit them. Uncle Sam was one of Mama's older brothers, and he owned a large grocery store.

Mama showed Uncle Sam around the apartment while Daddy and the girls sat in the living room.

"It's not a bad place," Uncle Sam said as he returned with Mama. Then he looked at Daddy and said, "Naturally, it's not as nice as the other one."

Daddy didn't answer, but Mama shrugged

her shoulders and said, "We just couldn't afford it. You know that, Sam."

For a moment no one spoke, and then Uncle Sam turned toward Daddy and said, "Harry, I could use another man in the store. How about working for me?"

Evidently he had discussed his plan with Mama, because she seemed to be the only one who wasn't surprised. She looked hopefully toward Daddy.

"No, thanks," Daddy answered quickly. "I have a job that I like. Working in a store just isn't for me."

"When a man has a wife and children to support," Uncle Sam insisted, "it's his duty to make a decent living for them, even if he has to work at something he isn't crazy about."

Amy looked fearfully at Daddy. She knew how quickly his temper came and went, and she saw his face growing angrier and angrier.

But before he could speak, Mama said sharply, "Just a minute, Harry." She turned toward Amy and Laura. "I want the two of you to get into your coats and hats and go outside and play."

Sullenly the girls walked into their bedroom. Why was it that they were always left out when anything interesting had to be discussed? They dawdled, pretending to be dressing, and they heard Daddy say angrily, "Now listen, Sam, I don't go around telling other people how to live their lives, and I'll thank you not to tell me how to live mine."

Mama's voice rose sharply above his. "Harry, you ought to be ashamed of yourself talking to Sam that way. He's just doing his best to see that we have more of the good things in life."

Amy knew that she was thinking about the piano that Uncle Sam had for his children, and how his boys had bicycles and went away to the country every summer. Amy and Laura didn't particularly care about having a piano or going away to the country, but for a long time they had been asking for bicycles.

As Mama spoke, the girls peeped through the French doors that divided their bedroom from the living room. Mama seemed to have forgotten all about them, and neither one of the two men noticed them watching.

After Mama finished speaking, Daddy didn't answer. He just hung his head, the way Amy and Laura did when they were scolded, and looked intently at his fingernails. He didn't seem to be angry at Uncle Sam anymore. He just sat there quietly. Mama watched him for a moment, and then suddenly she moved over to him. There were tears in her eyes, and she put her head on his shoulder and just said, "Oh, Harry!" in a tired voice. Daddy's arms went around her, and he was crying too. "I guess I haven't been a good husband to you," he said.

And then Mama was really crying. She said, "But it doesn't really matter not having all those fine things, does it, darling? I really don't want all those things." She was crying very hard. "We're so happy."

As soon as Mama started to cry, Amy and Laura both broke into tears. They put their arms around each other.

"Don't cry, Amy," Laura sobbed, kissing her. They ran into the room, and threw their arms around Mama and Daddy.

"I don't want a bicycle," Laura cried, "I hate bicycles."

"I hate them too," Amy yelled.

And then Daddy smiled even though he still had tears in his eyes, and Mama smiled even though she still had tears in her eyes.

"I hate bicycles too," Daddy said.

"And so do I," said Mama.

And then suddenly they were all laughing.

Uncle Sam had been sitting in the old arm-chair. He moved around uncomfortably, and his eyes didn't seem to know where to look. When the family started laughing, he sighed a little and rose from the chair. In a quiet voice, he said he thought he would be going.

Mama went over to him, kissed him, and thanked him. Daddy shook hands with him and apologized for being angry. But Laura and Amy ran out of the room. They hated him and they didn't want to say good-bye to him or kiss him.

Mama came after them. She said firmly, "Now you go back and kiss your uncle good-bye."

So they both went back to the room and said good-bye in growly voices. Uncle Sam hugged them, kissed them, and gave them each a dime. They weren't so angry with him after that.

Mama made franks and beans for supper that night, and Amy and Laura played their favorite game of "Faces" with Daddy. There was no face that Daddy couldn't make.

"Make a face of Abraham Lincoln!" Laura said.

Daddy passed his hands over his face, and Abraham Lincoln looked down at them. Daddy had sucked in his cheeks, drawn his mouth into a tight line, and had put a smiley look into his eyes.

Then Amy said in a delicious kind of way, because she knew what would happen, "Make a lion!"

Daddy's hands moved over his face, and the snarling face of a lion came out. A horrible roar rose from the lion's mouth, and the girls ran shrieking with pleasure from the room. A few minutes later they were back.

"Make Mama's face!" asked Laura.

The hands moved, and there was a smiling face with fluttering eyelashes.

"Now Laura!" commanded Amy, and in a second she saw a chubby face with full cheeks chewing away on bubble gum.

"Oh, I don't look like that," Laura cried, not at all pleased.

"You do too," laughed Amy. Daddy always changed his faces when he did Amy and Laura, and the girls never knew what would come out.

"Make Amy now, make Amy!" shouted Laura.

The hands moved, and there was a skinny little face crying.

"That's just the way you look when you cry," laughed Laura.

"No, I don't, not really," said Amy. "Do I, Daddy?"

But the hands were moving over the face again. The girls watched eagerly. What would it be: George Washington? Grandma? A tiger? What? The hands finished their trip, and a face appeared. They smiled. It was a nice face. It had a funny, crooked nose, shining blue eyes, and smiling lips. It was Daddy.

School

Monday morning Amy woke up before the alarm clock rang. On Saturdays, Sundays, or holidays she would jump right out of bed and dress herself as quickly as she could, anxious to make the most of the precious day. But on weekday mornings it took her a long time to get out of bed.

First she would pass her hands over her stomach, pressing here and there to see if she could find any parts that hurt. If she couldn't, she would then concentrate on her throat, swallowing hard to see if it weren't just a little bit sore. Usually she felt fine, and there was nothing that she could do but get up slowly, eat breakfast slowly, dress slowly, and walk very slowly to school.

Sometimes, though, she might say to Mama, "I don't feel so well."

Mama's face would look worried. "What hurts you?"

"Oh, it's not really that anything hurts me. I just don't feel so well." She would look hopefully at Mama.

But Mama always had the same answer. "It's up to you, Amy. If you really don't feel well, you can stay home. I can't see inside of you, so you'll have to make the decision."

Then Amy would grumble for a little while, but she would go to school just the same.

On this Monday morning, after Amy had checked her stomach and throat with particular care but no success, she poked Laura and whispered, "Laura, aren't you scared?"

Laura woke right up. She knew immediately what Amy meant.

"I just hope my teacher is all right," she said.

The girls whispered for a while. Laura said she hoped the boys and girls sat separately, not like in the old school. She told Amy she hated boys, "especially Peter Ross."

"I hope there's nobody like him in this school."

"Well, if you hated him so much," Amy said, "why did you used to walk past his house all the time on your way to school? It took twice as long that way."

"It did not," Laura cried.

"It did so," screamed Amy.

"It did not," roared Laura, and she socked Amy with a pillow.

"It did so, and you were in love with him. He was your boy friend," giggled Amy. Laura prepared to hit her again with the pillow, but Mama came into the room at that moment.

In a very little while the girls found themselves inside of the principal's office, ready to be taken up to their new classrooms.

When Amy walked into Room 208, and saw all the children's faces turned toward her, she began to get that sick, scared feeling in her stomach. The girl who brought her up from the office handed some papers to the teacher, and said something about a new girl. The room became very quiet, as the children listened and looked. As far as Amy was concerned, she thought that she had never seen so many peculiar and mean-looking faces in her life. A girl stood up in the back of the room, waved, and stuck out her tongue, and immediately Amy felt better. She and Cynthia in the same class. What luck!

As Mrs. Farber, the teacher, came toward her, Amy noticed how young and pretty she was, and what a pleasant smile she had. Mrs. Farber put an arm around Amy's shoulder and said, "We're very glad to have you, Amy, and I'm sure you're going to like being here in class 4B too."

Amy decided that she liked Mrs. Farber.

"Now where can we put you?" continued the teacher.

Amy looked anxiously toward the back of the room where Cynthia sat, and noticed an empty seat right next to her friend. This certainly was her lucky day.

"There's a seat back there," she said.

Mrs. Farber looked. Then she nodded and smiled at Amy. Amy smiled back and began to walk over to the seat when Mrs. Farber said suddenly, "But Amy, you're too small to sit so far back."

Amy decided that she didn't like Mrs. Farber after all. It was bad enough that she couldn't sit next to Cynthia, but to make matters worse, Mrs. Farber had to go and announce to everybody that she was small. Amy stopped smiling. "Leave it to grown-ups!" she thought. "They just don't seem to have any sense, and they always manage to say the wrong thing."

Mrs. Farber asked all the children in the second row, from the third seat on, to move one seat back.

"You can sit in that seat," she said. "I think that's close enough for you to see. Of course," Mrs. Farber smiled, "you are quite petite, but we can always move you up later if you can't see."

Amy had no idea what "petite" meant, but she hardly thought it was flattering. She noticed all the children watching her, and she began to feel like Tom Thumb. Grownups! She sulked over to her desk, and let the seat down with a bang. In the old school they had only nice teachers, except of course for Mrs. Stein, Miss O'Brien, Miss Anderson, and maybe a few others. She certainly never had to put up with anything like this crazy teacher, who just seemed to wait for any opportunity to tell the whole world that she, Amy, was small.

She glared around the room and eyed with distaste the drawings hanging up on the walls. Look at that silly Indian drawing! He looked like a sack of potatoes. Why, she could draw lots better than that. Her eyes traveled over to the window where a whole row of bright geranium plants arched their red heads. They wouldn't last long. That one in the middle was dying already.

A little patch of sunlight played on her desk, and Amy looked at it with hatred. She knew that sooner or later it would be in her eyes. Then she would have to twist and turn her head and squint until the teacher told someone to pull up the shade. Nine chances out of ten, the shade would be broken, as it always seemed to be in the other school. She would just have to suffer in silence until the sunlight moved over and started annoying the child next to her. She glanced over at the girl sitting on her right side, and immediately her anger disappeared.

The girl had the most beautiful hair that Amy had ever seen. Her eyes traveled down the long, shining black braids adoringly, until they reached the perky red ribbons at the end. What hair! In all the fairy-tale books that Amy read so avidly, she always dismissed with impatience the suggestion that princesses had blond hair. Ridiculous! Rapunzel, for instance, wouldn't really be Rapunzel for Amy unless she sat sadly at the window of the high tower with her long, sleek black braids, maybe tied with red ribbons, hanging straight down the stone walls. Those illustrations that they had in some of her books really annoyed her with their blond, blue-eyed heroines. She found that the pictures she made up in her own mind were usually much more satisfying.

She continued to stare at the lovely hair until the girl turned her head and stared back at Amy. Her eyes were very black, as black as her hair, and her skin was dark. She looked seriously at Amy, and Amy smiled. For a moment nothing happened. The same serious face looked back at her, and Amy began to feel embarrassed. But then the girl's lips moved, and she smiled quickly and turned away her head. "I'll tell her later what I think of her hair," Amy thought.

The girl behind Amy suddenly poked her. This was a signal that she recognized immediately, as did any child who had arrived at the fourth grade. She slid her arm along the seat, carefully watching Mrs. Farber up front, who was telling the children about Peter Stuyvesant. She stretched her arm back as far as it could go and cupped her hand. A piece of paper dropped into it, and slowly Amy drew her hand back until it was hidden underneath her desk. A note lay in her hand, folded over but with nothing, of course, written on the outside. An experienced note passer never writes names on a note, lest it be captured by the enemy. A quick poke and a low whisper are all that is necessary to direct a note to its destination.

Amy glued her eyes on Mrs. Farber and tried to bring an interested, thoughtful look into her face as she carefully opened the note. She was very experienced at this business of note-passing, and she knew how suspicious teachers became when they saw you looking under your desk. She wrinkled her forehead to give Mrs. Farber the impression that she was concentrating on Peter Stuyvesant. Meanwhile she brought her arms up, and rested her hands upon the desk. The note lay open on the desk, and her hands surrounded it like a wall. Slowly she glanced down, as if she were looking at her hands while seriously thinking about Peter Stuyvesant. She read the note. It said:

"You are a dope, from Guess Who?"

Amy smiled happily. She knew that Cynthia had sent the note, and nothing at that moment could have pleased her more than those four friendly words of welcome. Casually Amy drew a pencil from her pencil case. She held it lightly in one hand and rested it against her mouth to really give the impression of a studious child. But this was the time for speed. When Mrs. Farber looked toward another part of the room, Amy was ready. Quickly she wrote under the message:

"You are a dope too, and so is Mrs. Farber."

By the time Mrs. Farber looked again in her direction, Amy had laid the pencil down and had twisted her mouth into a serious frown. She had also learned from her experience that an observant teacher will be more suspicious of a bright smile than a thoughtful frown.

Again Amy's hands moved beneath the desk, gently folding the note. The operation completed, she raised her hand behind her head, scratching it thoughtfully, and dropping the note on the desk behind her. She had no doubt that the note would reach Cynthia, and would return in a matter of time.

The girl next to her, with the beautiful braids, stood up and began to speak in answer to a question from Mrs. Farber about Peter Stuyvesant. Her voice was soft and pleasant, but Amy could see at once that she must have come from another country. She hesitated as she spoke, stumbling frequently over the words. From time to time Mrs. Farber would stop her to correct something that she had said. All around her, Amy could hear soft giggles whenever the girl made a mistake. She watched the girl's face sympathetically as it grew redder and redder, and she noticed the girl's trembling hand gripping the side of the desk.

When Rosa, for that was her name, said, "The Dutch people was combing over to America," instead of "The Dutch people came to America," some of the children laughed out loud. Rosa's face turned scarlet, and Amy thought angrily about how mean kids could be. She longed to reach over and take that trembling hand. She wanted to tell Rosa not to worry, that soon she would be able to speak very well, and she shouldn't mind those silly kids.

Mrs. Farber spoke sharply to the class. "I don't see anything funny," she said, "and I think you're all behaving like a bunch of kindergarten babies and not fourth-graders."

When Mrs. Farber said that, all the children stopped laughing. They felt insulted that she could compare them to kindergarten babies. Mrs. Farber looked sternly at the class for a few moments, and it seemed as if she wanted to say something else to them. She must have changed her mind though, because she turned back to Rosa and said gently, "All right, dear, you may sit down."

Another girl was called upon, and as she began to recite, Amy tried to catch Rosa's eye. She wanted to smile and nod at her, and show her that there was at least one person in the class who was on her side. But Rosa's eyes remained glued on her desk.

In the course of the morning, Amy's note returned to her. This time it said, "You look like this:"

Amy grinned delightedly. Well, she would fix Cynthia. She worked carefully, and when she had finished, the note said, "You look like this:"

Again Amy scratched her head, and again the note fell on the desk behind her.

About a half-hour before noon, Mrs. Farber said that since it was such a sunny day they could all get their coats and hats, and go down to the yard for a recess. The first row stood up and started filing into the clothes closet. The children seemed quite orderly and well-behaved as they stepped into the clothes closet and as they stepped out, but Amy knew what was happening inside.

By the time the children in her row stepped inside, wearing the same law-abiding expressions on their faces, the floor of the closet was already lined with coats and hats. More coats and hats dropped to the floor as the children charged around inside. A hat went zooming by Amy's ear, and as she started to giggle, somebody threw a coat over her head. She giggled some more and threw the coat over someone else's head. It didn't matter that she was not yet acquainted with any of the children in her row. Inside the clothes closet you didn't wait for formal introductions. All you had to do to make friends was to throw around articles of clothing, preferably belonging to someone not in the same row.

By the time Amy found her own coat and hat, she was very breathless. Nevertheless, she managed to make her face appear innocent and respectable as she stepped out of the closet.

Once they were down in the yard, the class divided. The boys went off to play punch ball, and the girls remained together discussing what they should do.

"Let's play punch ball," Cynthia said.

Amy knew that Cynthia wanted to play the same kind of games the boys played.

"I'd rather jump rope," said a blond girl named Ellen.

Some of the other girls also said they wanted to jump rope, and a group of them went off together. Amy watched them moving away. She really wanted to go along with them, but she supposed Cynthia would be annoyed if she did. Punch ball just wasn't the kind of game she liked. Maybe if she could hit the ball more often, she would get used to it.

Cynthia and another girl named Sally said that they would be the captains for the two teams. There were ten other girls who were going to play, and the teams were formed by each captain taking turns at picking a girl for her side. Amy always dreaded this part most of all. She hated standing there waiting to be picked, and trying hard to look as if it really didn't matter whether she was picked first or last. But it really did matter.

Seldom had Amy ever been picked first, but she knew how proudly the first one walked over to the side of the captain, and how admiringly the eyes of the others followed her. But when you were picked last, you had to stand there while one by one the group of waiting girls grew smaller and smaller, until only you were left all alone. Then you and everyone else knew that you were the least important and the least wanted. Amy hoped hard that it wouldn't happen to her this time, as so often it had.

Cynthia chose first. She called on Harriet, a tall, heavy-set girl who, Amy knew, would be able to hit the ball better than anyone else. Sally chose Marcia. Now it was Cynthia's turn again. Amy turned a pleading look on her friend. If Cynthia would only look toward her, she would understand how important it was for her to be picked. But Cynthia quickly chose Roslyn, a wiry girl with well-developed muscles on her legs. Amy watched Roslyn shrug her shoulders and walk over to Cynthia's side. Some people, she realized, never worried about being picked. Girls like Roslyn and Harriet probably never even thought about it. Only people like herself, who knew what it meant to stand alone like the cheese in the "Farmer in the Dell," ever had to think and worry about it.

Sally called Bernice over to her side, and again it was Cynthia's turn. This time Cynthia looked right at her and said, "Amy."

"It really doesn't matter," Amy thought as she walked over to Cynthia's side, "being picked first, as long as it isn't last." She watched the remaining group of girls with pity and thought happily about her friend — her best friend, Cynthia — who had rescued her.

Her eyes moved away from the girls and wandered around the schoolyard. Over on one side, the boys were well into the game of punch ball. She saw the girls jumping rope, and heard them chanting:

Dolly Dimple walks like this
Dolly Dimple talks like this
Dolly Dimple throws a kiss
Dolly Dimple misses like this.

The yard seemed full of movement and excitement to Amy. But over against the wire school fence stood a girl who had nothing to do with the movement and excitement, a girl who stood all alone. Amy looked with envy at the girl's long black braids tied with bright red ribbons, but when she saw Rosa's winter coat, old and faded, and too long in the sleeves, she thought painfully of her own coat, and sympathized. She realized how lonely Rosa must be and how difficult it must be for her to make friends. At least she had Cynthia. "Well," she thought, "I can fix that."

"I'm going over to ask Rosa to play with us," Amy announced.

Cynthia looked around the yard until she saw Rosa leaning against the fence. "What for?' she asked.

All the girls looked toward Amy, and she felt uncomfortable.

"Well," she said, "she's probably too shy to ask us if she can play. You know she can't speak too well."

"I'll say she can't," Cynthia laughed. " 'When the Dutch people was combing over to America,' " she imitated. She made her voice sound high-pitched, and she walked around the girls with little mincing steps and a sad expression on her face. All the girls, including Amy, started to laugh. Not only did Cynthia sound like Rosa, but she even looked like her. Cynthia laughed too.

"She's so funny," she said.

"Oh, she can't help it," Amy said quietly. "She'll learn how to talk in a little while."

"Who cares?" Cynthia answered. "I don't like her, and who wants a girl like that around anyway? Now let's get the game started. I'll choose you for who's up first," she said to Sally.

While the girls were choosing, Amy looked over toward Rosa again. Cynthia was probably right, but as she watched Rosa, a strong feeling of pity grew inside her. "If we're up first, I'll go over and talk to her while I'm waiting for my turn," she thought.

"O.K.," Cynthia said, throwing an arm around Amy's shoulder, "we're up first. Let's go."

The girls walked over to "Home," and Amy wondered if Cynthia would be angry if she spoke to Rosa. Cynthia's arm on her shoulder made her proud and happy. She didn't want Cynthia ever to be mad at her.

Harriet was up first. As Amy waited, she avoided looking toward Rosa. "I can speak to her later," she thought. But instead of feeling better, she felt annoyed and angry, and she didn't know why. She was glad when her turn came. Nothing seemed more important at that moment than hitting the ball, and hitting it hard.

The Park

"What!" exclaimed Cynthia in surprise. "You never heard of Crotona Park?"

"No," confessed Amy.

"And you never heard about Indian Rock either?"

"No-o-o," faintly answered Amy, very, very ashamed of her own ignorance.

"Well," continued Cynthia, "you just don't know anything about this neighborhood until you go over to Crotona Park and climb up on Indian Rock."

The two girls were walking home from school, one arm of each entwined around the other's shoulder.

"What's Indian Rock?" Amy asked.

Cynthia smiled and nestled her head closer to Amy's ear as she prepared to let her friend into the secret. She whispered as she unfolded her story; although no one was around to hear.

"Indian Rock is a rock that the Indians used to use as a lookout. It's right in the middle of the park, and there are holes on one side of it that the Indians made so they could climb up to the top." Cynthia's voice became even lower and more mysterious. "I think maybe they even used to have human sacrifices on it."

"How do you know?" whispered Amy.

"Because if you look real close — " Cynthia paused and stared intently at her friend, as if she wondered whether this piece of information might better be left unsaid. Amy held her breath, and finally Cynthia continued, " — you can see bloodstains."

"Oh!" breathed Amy, amazed and horrified, but not at all doubtful of Cynthia's story.

"Can we go this afternoon?" she begged, still in a whisper.

Cynthia agreed. As soon as they reached home, Amy hurried inside. She changed from her blouse and skirt into her accustomed slacks and sweater without even waiting for Mama to tell her. While she gulped down her milk and cookies, she told Mama and Laura all about the park and Indian Rock.

"Sounds like a lot of baloney to me," commented Laura.

"It is not," cried Amy indignantly. "Is it, Mama?"

But Mama's mind seemed to be on other matters, as it so often was. "Just be careful when you cross the street," she replied, "and be home in time for supper."

Amy dashed out of the house, and called for Cynthia. Impatiently she waited while Cynthia's mother slowly resewed all of the buttons on her daughter's coat. She twisted in her seat as Cynthia's mother lectured Cynthia about losing buttons, reminding her, it seemed to Amy, about every single button she had ever lost from the time she first started wearing buttons. Amy couldn't control her impatience any longer.

"I'll wait for you outside," she announced, and marched out of the house.

She stood on Cynthia's stoop and felt her fingers growing stiff inside of her mittens. When she breathed, smoke came from her mouth and nostrils. She puffed big circles from her mouth, the way Daddy did with his cigar, and she watched the stream of smoke as it unfolded and joined with the cold air. It would snow soon. The radio had said so, and Mama said so. Hopefully Amy looked up at the gray sky.

"If it snows today," she thought, "tomorrow we can really have fun."

Amy knew that on the first day of snow, all one could do was admire, and wait impatiently for the next day. On the first day, the snow lay soft and white and evenly all over the sidewalks and streets. If you picked it up in your hands and tried to shape a snowball, it just crumbled away and dropped like sand through your fingers. But on the next day, if it had snowed heavily, the sanitation trucks would come through and push the snow in the streets to either side. Then huge mounds of hardening gray snow would divide the sidewalk from the street all the way down the block. Grownups generally complained about it. They said it was a disgrace, and that the snow should be removed right away so that a person didn't have to wade through mountains of snow just to cross the street.

But Amy loved those snow mounds. Their appearance meant that she and the other children would have real snowball fights, using opposite mounds as forts. It meant, in more peaceful times, that they could make little houses out of the grimy snow heaps, hollowing out the middle part, and, if the top didn't fall in, sit inside as long as they liked.

So far this season there had been no snow, and right now there was no sign of it either. There was also no sign of Cynthia. Amy stamped her feet, partly because she was so annoyed and impatient, and partly to keep them warm. Should she ring Cynthia's bell? she wondered. She would. Back she went into the hall, and nearly bumped into Cynthia, who came charging down the stairs, a sulky expression on her face.

"My mother always picks on me," she complained.

Amy nodded sympathetically and linked her arm through Cynthia's. The two girls hurried along the street, determined that nothing now should stop them.

But as they stood on Boston Road waiting to cross the big street, another interruption, in the shape of Annette DeLuca developed. Annette sat in Amy's row in school, and from the little that Amy had seen of her, she had decided that she didn't like her. Annette was too good for Amy's tastes, too polite, too ladylike; and besides, she was teacher's pet. Her clothes, too, annoyed Amy. They were so beautiful that they only reminded her the more of her own ill-fitting hand-me-downs. Today Annette wore a snow-white angora beret, and a bright red coat with two rows of gold buttons down the front.

When she saw the two girls, she smiled warmly at Amy and said very pleasantly, "Hello, Amy."

"Hello," returned Amy less pleasantly. She

looked at Cynthia, surprised at first that she and Annette did not exchange greetings. Well, of course, she realized, Cynthia couldn't possibly like that kind of girl. In amazement, she heard her friend speak in a faint, pleading voice.

"Hello, Annette."

Annette didn't reply. She continued to smile at Amy.

"Where are you going, Amy?" she asked.

Before Amy could answer, Cynthia spoke again, more pleadingly than before. "Oh, come on, Annette. Don't be mad. I'm sorry, and I won't do it again."

Amy stared in surprise at the two girls. Why, here was her glorious Cynthia actually begging someone to be friends with her, and that someone a girl like Annette. She saw Cynthia's face turned adoringly toward Annette, and all of Amy's amazement turned to jealousy. She did not like Annette one bit. In fact, at that moment, she disliked her more than anyone else, even more than Hitler, who, Daddy said, had made so much trouble in the world.

Annette spoke, still smiling at Amy. "I can't hear anything she says. She's just speaking to the wall when she says anything to me."

Amy looked around desperately and saw

the traffic light change. "Come on," she said to Cynthia, "let's go. Good-bye, Annette."

But Cynthia held her arm. "Tell her what I said," she commanded.

"She heard you," Amy grumbled.

"No I didn't," smiled Annette.

"Go on, tell her," poked Cynthia.

Amy felt the whole day was ruined. She glared at Annette and said quickly, "She says she's sorry and she won't do it again, and she wants you not to be mad at her."

Annette deliberated for a moment. "You can tell her that she's been fresh just once too often," she finally replied. "I told her that I would never speak to her as long as I live, and I won't."

"Tell her *please*," poked Cynthia again.

All of the feelings of jealousy and hatred exploded suddenly in Amy. "Just a minute," she barked. She pulled Cynthia away and whispered in her ear, "I'm going home. I don't want to go to the park anymore."

"Why, what's the matter?" asked Cynthia innocently.

"You know. I don't like that girl, and I don't know why you want to be friends with her," Amy whined. "You're *my* friend."

"Sure I am," Cynthia said soothingly, patting Amy's shoulder. "And if you tell her to be friends with me, I promise I'll be your best friend as long as I live."

Cynthia's promise made the thought of sharing her with someone else a little less painful. She allowed Cynthia to draw her back to where Annette stood. Cynthia prodded her, and she said reluctantly, "Come on, Annette, make up with her."

Annette shrugged her shoulders. "Let's just not talk about it anymore," she said, flashing her friendly smile. "Where are you going now?"

"The park," muttered Amy.

"Ask her if she wants to come," whispered Cynthia.

"You want to come with us?" Amy asked doubtfully.

Annette drew her arm through Amy's and said, "Well, I'll come with you, but not with her."

The girls crossed the street, arms linked, with Amy in the center. As far as Amy was concerned there was one arm too many, and she thought bitterly, "Two's company, three's a crowd." She hated the way Annette chattered about herself, her clothes, her dog, her brother, and all sorts of dumb things. She hated the way Cynthia listened eagerly to everything she said, laughed heartily at all her silly jokes, and looked so admiringly at her. She never looked that way at Amy, and sometimes she didn't even listen when Amy spoke. Only the thought of Indian Rock made Amy feel that something pleasant might develop during the afternoon.

The girls turned a corner, and Crotona Park lay before Amy's eyes.

"Where's Indian Rock?" she asked, interrupting Annette, who was describing a new taffeta dress. Cynthia's eyes remained fixed on Annette's face.

"Oh, you'll see it soon," she said impatiently.

Annette began chattering again, and Amy peered eagerly around her. She expected Indian Rock to loom up suddenly in front of her, huge, black, and with red streams of dried-up blood. She walked quickly, forcing the others to keep up with her, and as she listened to Annette's voice the thought of human sacrifices seemed almost pleasant to her.

"There it is," said Cynthia.

Amy's eyes followed the extended finger and saw Indian Rock for the first time. It was a large gray rock sitting all by itself on a little hill.

"Is that it?" Amy asked, very disappointed. It looked like such an ordinary rock, not nearly as large as she had expected.

"Sure," said Cynthia. She gripped Amy's arm a little tighter, and continued confidentially, "See, Amy, doesn't it look like a bull's head from here?"

Annette laughed scornfully. "It looks like a pumpkin," she announced.

To Amy, it looked like a rock, just that — a large gray rock. But she couldn't let her friend down, so she squinted her eyes, held her head to one side, and thought to herself, "It looks like a bull's head, it looks like a bull's head." And all of a sudden that was exactly what it looked like.

"It looks like a bull's head," she said coldly to Annette.

"Well, maybe it does look like a pumpkin," said the faithless Cynthia. "But let's hurry up. There's no one on it now."

They walked very quickly, and the rock became larger and larger, until just as they could almost put out their hands and touch it two boys dashed ahead of them, ran around the side of the rock where the holes were, and scurried up to the top. Amy could see that only three or four children could fit on top. But who would want to sit up there with boys? They would just have to wait until the boys decided to come down; but judging from the way they sprawled out on the rock, it seemed likely that they planned to remain up there a long time.

"Now listen," Cynthia called up to them, "we were here first."

"Blah, blah, blah," laughed the boys.

"You better get off there," shouted Cynthia, clenching her fists, "or I'll make you."

"You and who else?" sneered the bigger boy, who seemed their own age.

"O.K., you asked for it," roared Cynthia. She turned to the two girls who stood staunchly beside her and motioned them a short distance away. "Come over here; I've got an idea."

"What are you going to do?" whispered Amy after they had withdrawn.

"We'll give them three to get off, and then if the don't we'll collect some of these little pebbles all over the ground and throw them at the boys. The pebbles won't really hurt them, and they won't be able to fight back because they don't have any ammunition up there. They'll get down pretty fast, don't worry."

She began laughing and soon Amy and Annette were giggling too. Evidently Annette was so pleased and excited by the plan that she forgot to ask Amy to repeat what Cynthia said.

Some tall trees grew around one side of the rock, and the girls ran behind them so that the boys could not see what they were doing. They filled their pockets with pebbles, and then they took off their hats — Annette even took off her white beret — and they filled them with pebbles too. Cynthia suggested that they fill up their mittens, and they did. Soon all was ready. They held their hats and mittens behind their backs and marched over to the rock. The boys had not moved.

"You back again," one of them said.

"O.K.," said Cynthia, "we'll give you three to get off, or you'll be sorry."

"If I get off here, *you'll* be sorry," threatened the older boy.

"O-o-o-o-ne," cried Cynthia, stretching the word out.

The boys squirmed uncomfortably, but remained at their post.

"Two-o-o," drawled Cynthia. The girls gripped their hats tightly, prepared to fire at the right moment.

"Two and a half," Cynthia recited happily.

Amy and Annette giggled, and the boys laughed a little shakily and said, "Blah, blah, blah."

"Two and three quarters," yelled Cynthia.

"This is your last chance. Are you getting off or not?"

"Just try and make us," came the gallant reply.

"Three," roared Cynthia.

Three hats were produced, and fistfuls of pebbles began flying. When the girls had emptied out their hats, they dug into their pockets. The boys were surprised at this sudden attack. At first they put up their arms in front of their faces, but as the pebbles kept coming, the younger boy started to cry.

"Crybaby, crybaby," chanted Cynthia, and the others joined in. Finally the two boys scampered down from the rock and ran, with the pebbles still flying after them.

"We'll get even," cried the big boy as he ran. "We'll fix you."

"Blah, blah, blah," shouted Cynthia, emptying her mittens of the last handful of pebbles. They continued throwing pebbles at the retreating figures even after they were out of range. It was fun.

"Well, let's get on," Cynthia said a little breathlessly.

Annette climbed up first. Cynthia showed Amy the three holes in the rock that the Indians had made as steps. You put your fingers first into the second hole so you could pull yourself up to the first. From then on it was easy to get to the top. And what a view, Amy thought. The few times she had been to the country, she had gone with her family to look at the view from various famous mountains. But all she had seen were other mountains and lakes. Here, just about the whole park lay before her delighted eyes. She saw the handball courts on one side of the park and the playground on the other. How tiny the people looked, like little dots of color! Down the hill on which the rock stood, Amy saw the dusty green waters of Indian Lake. In the summer, Cynthia said, you could row there or fish; and in the winter, if the lake froze over and you had a pair of ice skates, you could go skating.

"This is the nicest park I ever saw," Amy said happily, and the girls agreed with her.

They sat quietly for a while, talking gleefully about how they had routed the enemy. They dangled their feet over the side, and Cynthia showed them how she could slide off the rock by lying face down on the top, gripping one of the edges, and then sliding her body off until she hung suspended on one side of the rock. Then she jumped. Annette could do it too, and Amy decided to try. She managed to slide her body over the side, but as she dangled there, still holding on to the top, her courage ebbed. When she looked down, the ground seemed very far away.

"Come on, jump!" Cynthia ordered.

Amy's fingers remained glued to the top. "Please get me off," she whimpered.

Annette and Cynthia giggled, but they grabbed her legs and pulled her down.

"Sissy," Cynthia said.

Next they played "King of the Mountain." The person who was king sat up on top of Indian Rock, and the object of the game was to keep anyone else from climbing up. If anyone did manage to reach the top, she became the new king. They played the game for a long time, until Annette's white hat had turned a deep gray, and Amy's nose boasted a new scratch, and a new rip had appeared in Cynthia's slacks.

"Whew, I'm tired," complained Annette. "Let's just sit on the top for a while."

Hot and red-faced, they climbed up again. They hadn't been sitting there long when they heard a rustling from the trees.

"Enemy approaching," Cynthia said.

Seven boys emerged from behind the trees, two of whom were the original boys on the rock.

"Uh, uh, looks like trouble," said Annette.

"Don't worry," comforted the fearless Cynthia. "They won't get us off. If they start to throw pebbles, just put your head down between your knees and put your arms over your face. We'll stick our legs over the edge, and if they try to climb up we can kick them."

The boys surrounded the rock. Their hands were hidden inside their jackets, and the girls noticed uncomfortably how suspiciously their jackets bulged.

"All right, you smart alecks," said the boy whom they had chased away, "now you get off there or you'll really be sorry."

"Sticks and stones can break my bones, but words can never harm me," said Amy, surprised at her own bravery, but confident with Cynthia there. The other girls started chanting it too, as loudly as they could, so that the boy's voice was drowned out.

They saw him motion to the other boys, and suddenly the hands inside the jackets emerged, holding familiar and deadly objects. In a moment the girls found themselves wet, although it wasn't raining. Horrified, they looked into the muzzles of seven water pistols. They saw that the boys, evidently expecting a long siege, had also brought along seven milk bottles filled with water. Only one defense remained to them, and that was immediate flight.

Annette scrambled down first. Cynthia slid

off second, and Amy climbed down third — much faster, if she had thought about it, than she would have believed possible. By the time she reached the ground, her friends had already covered quite a distance. Annette, who in spite of her ladylike appearance had a strong pair of legs, was leading. Prancing behind her came Cynthia.

"Wait for me! Wait for me!" shrieked Amy, but her disloyal friends did not even turn their heads. She started to run, and the boys dropped their bottles and followed in hot pursuit. Poor Amy, she never could run quickly. Her skinny legs always felt as if they had lead in them, and her breath came hard and choky in her throat. It was over almost as soon as it began. Amy found herself surrounded by seven unfriendly faces. Some of the boys wanted to catch the other two, but they finally decided that one out of three was not a terribly bad percentage.

Amy's stomach turned flip-flops. She knew that there could be no revenge crueler, no humiliation greater, no torture fiercer than that dreamed up by BOYS. A short but beautiful daydream rose in her mind. Perhaps her friends would return with reinforcements. Perhaps Laura would lead the returning forces. Perhaps, perhaps . . . But off in the distance Amy could just barely make out two tiny figures moving quickly in the opposite direction.

The boys held a powwow concerning their prisoner. Some of them wanted to tie her to a tree and do an Indian war dance around her, while others maintained that they should empty the remains of their water pistols on her.

What should she do? She knew from her reading how her favorite heroes and heroines behaved when confronted with a cruel and merciless enemy. She knew how they held their heads up proudly, how they refused to humble themselves before their foe, and how their courage, even in the face of unbelievable tortures, did not waver for a moment. The boys drew around her, and she spoke.

"It wasn't my idea," she whimpered. "The other two girls thought it all up about throwing the pebbles."

"You threw them too," said the younger boy. "You didn't have to if you didn't want to."

"You better let me go," Amy continued to whimper, "or I'll tell my sister on you."

"Who's afraid of your sister?" said one of the boys. "I know what we should do with her. Make her go under the mill."

"No, I won't," yelled Amy, "and you can't make me."

But the boys lined up, one behind the other with their legs spread apart. One of the boys grabbed Amy and pushed her down between the legs of the first boy on the line. He began paddling her as hard as he could. There was nothing else she could do but crawl under the outstretched legs. She began crying, and one of the boys said uncomfortably, "Aw, let's go. She's just a crybaby."

They left her sprawled out on the ground and ran off shouting, "Crybaby, crybaby!"

How she hated boys! How she hated everything: the park, the neighborhood, Cynthia, Annette, everything! Finally she stood up and began rubbing her back. She was cold and wet, and she hurt in the worst place of all. Whimpering a little, she started walking toward home, thinking about how she would tell Mama and Daddy that they would have to move right away.

It grew dark, and the lights in the park suddenly lit up. She gazed around fearfully, and found herself all alone in the middle of this strange, frightening place. She hurried along, sniffing and wishing desperately for Laura or Mama. Something soft fell on her nose, and then on her forehead. She stopped walking for a moment and stood quietly in the darkening, silent park. Just for a moment though, for the silence was broken by Amy's laughter.

She held out her arms, hands cupped inside her mittens, and caught them, soft and white, and like no other thing. She did not say it or even think it, but she felt it in every part of her that nothing, nothing at all in this world, can match the beauty and wonder of the first snowflakes of the year.

Mama

The snow fell for two days. With equal care
it covered the cracked pavements, the garbage cans, and the rooftops of the street. On
the third morning when Amy awoke, the snow
had stopped falling. Outside her window, it
had risen on the ledge up past the lower frame
and could be seen through the glass. Carefully she opened the window from the bottom,
so that the little snow ridge on the ledge might
remain intact. She poked her fingers into it,
and saw with pleasure that the snow had
hardened and did not crumble around the
holes her fingers had made.

The coming of the cold weather served as a
signal to the prudent housewives of the street.
Mama, as well as practically every other
woman in the neighborhood, turned off her
refrigerator and stored the food in a window
box out on the fire escape. All through the
long winter the refrigerator door hung

strangely ajar, a sign of all the money being saved on electric bills.

In the morning, when Mama opened the kitchen window, Amy and Laura saw how the snow just about covered the box. As Mama quickly brushed it away, a blast of freezing air invaded the warm kitchen, and she said to the girls, "Wait inside until I can close the window."

When Amy and Laura returned the butter and milk stood on the table, and Mama smiled as she showed them what had happened to the milk during the night. A frozen column of white rose up from the top of each bottle, carrying the cardboard cover up along with it. Whenever a strong frost hit the city, the milk reacted in the same way. It seemed as if some generous milkman had put too much milk into the bottle, but for some strange reason the milk did not overflow.

On this morning the children hardly minded going to school. It meant a slow, glorious walk through the snow. In many places no one had walked as yet, and great patches of unbroken white spread out just crying for footprints. Amy and Laura left their house very early, anxious to be the first to put their footprints into the empty spaces. They walked slowly, stamping their feet, and making different designs in the snow.

Laura could make beautiful trees. She would walk with both feet very close together in a straight line to make the trunk of the tree. Then she made the branches by walking in different directions from the trunk. After that, she could make leaves by taking off her mittens and stamping her handprints all around the branches. She made wonderful trees, but they were never there on the way back.

On Boston Road, a sanitation truck slowly lumbered along, reminding the children of the snowball fights in store for them that afternoon. Already the snow could be shaped, and by the time Amy and Laura reached the school their fingers under their mittens smarted from contact with the cold snow. The white, powdery blobs on the front, sides, and back of their coats announced the first engagement in the warfare that would continue until the last piece of snow had disappeared.

How could they be expected to line up quietly and patiently on such a day, and march silently up the stairs to their classrooms? If someone slid some cold snow down your back, how could you be expected to remain in line and not howl and wiggle?

In Amy's class, the activity inside of the clothes closet reflected the excitement of the day. There was even more charging around than usual, while galoshes, hats, and coats flew in all directions. At lunchtime it would be a miracle if anyone could find two of the same galoshes without a considerable amount of frantic searching. So great became the hub-bub, and so long did the children take to hang up their coats, that Mrs. Farber suspiciously approached the clothes closet. Just as she put her face through the door, Amy flung one of Dorothy Pinsky's galoshes at Rosalie Cooper. The flying boot whizzed by Mrs. Farber's astonished face.

"Well!" said Mrs. Farber. "Now who threw that?"

No reply issued from the darkness of the closet. Only for reasons of self-preservation would one member of the class squeal on an-other. Mrs. Farber gazed at the littered floor of the clothes closet and realized that one person alone could not be responsible for all that havoc.

"I am really surprised at this class," announced Mrs. Farber angrily. "I want the children in the closet now to pick up all the coats and hats and hang them up, and I want no more of this nonsense. Do you understand? Otherwise the whole class will stay in this afternoon."

A low, rebellious murmur arose from the children in the closet. It was true that they were partly responsible for the mess on the floor, but only partly. After all, the preceding rows had contributed their bit too, and they did not see why they should be singled out to establish order.

However, Mrs. Farber's threat of keeping the class in after school struck so much terror into all hearts that no protest was made. Ordinarily no one minded too much staying after school. Teachers always seemed to think it a horrible punishment, but actually Amy and her friends usually enjoyed it very much. It meant that everybody had to sit very quietly in their seats with their hands folded on their desks and look sadly toward the front of the room where the teacher sat. Whenever the teacher turned her head for a moment, the children would look at each other, make faces, and giggle. The most fun of all was when the teacher looked back again, and the children had to get their faces looking sad and serious again. Sometimes a child couldn't change his face fast enough, and the teacher would say, "There's nothing funny, Robert Goldstein," or, "If you think this is so funny, Pearl Anderson, maybe we'll all stay in again tomorrow." Once, in the old school, a teacher kept the class in for a whole week because they had thrown around board erasers when she was out of the room. What fun that had been! All the children had enjoyed it so much that they were sorry they didn't have to stay in the following week too.

But today, with the snow lying ripe and hard on the ground, no one wanted to stay in. By three o'clock the excitement had reached its height, and the children came pouring, galloping, and shrieking out of the quiet school. A film of ice had formed over the streets and sidewalks, and Amy went sliding along with the other children, falling every so often on the hard ground. She and Cynthia laid their plans for the afternoon, and even Laura agreed to join them. They would choose their fort and put a flag on it with a skull and crossbones, and then let anyone dare to attack them.

When they reached the street, Amy and Laura were surprised not to find Mama standing outside waiting for them, as she always did. Every day, except when it rained, Mama waited for them, and the first thing they looked for was her familiar figure. Even at a distance they could recognize the green crocheted beret, the old black coat, and when she waved to them, those bright red wool gloves. Of all Mama's clothes, the girls liked those gloves the best. As long as they could remember, Mama had worn them; and every year she spoke about throwing them out, but she never did. They were very long and ended in a bright green border that lay hidden under the sleeve of her coat. Two of the fingers were darned.

But today no welcoming figure stood in the front of the house. The girls felt annoyed as well as surprised, because they liked things to be as they always were. Seeing Mama after school always meant a warm hug and kiss, and after that cookies and milk.

Buster was there to greet them, though. He stood shivering on the top landing of the steps, barking expectantly at the children who hurried past on their way home from school. "He must know something's up," thought Amy, as she stooped down on her side of the gate and put her face close to the bars for Buster to lick.

"Silly, old pussy-cat dog," she cooed, putting an arm through the gate and patting his head. Buster barked and ran around the small landing. "Wish I could come in," Amy sighed. She and Buster had become very good friends by now. Hardly a day passed that they did not exchange confidences and, when conditions were favorable, share a pretzel too.

"Mr. Williams is a meany," she said. "Why won't he let me come in and play with you?" Buster whimpered sympathetically. This me-on-one-side-of-the-gate-and-you-on-the-other certainly didn't add anything to their friendship.

But this was no time to air old grievances. "I'll see you later, doggy, and don't forget to root for me." Another wet lick of his tongue on her face, and off she went to join Laura, who was casting appraising looks up and down the street.

They lingered for a few moments outside the house, considering the various snow mounds and discussing the possibilities of each one. They finally decided on one farther down the block, and hurried inside to change their clothes and claim their site before anyone else.

Mama was not inside. Instead, they found Aunt Minnie, one of Daddy's older sisters, a widow who lived by herself.

"Hello, Amy, Laura," said Aunt Minnie, kissing them. "There's some cocoa waiting for you. Sit down and drink it while it's hot."

The cocoa smell filled the air delightfully, but there was something wrong, something missing.

"Where's Mama?" asked Amy.

Aunt Minnie looked away for a moment. The girls saw that she was uncomfortable, and Amy said again, this time whimpering a little, "Where's Mama?"

"Yes, where's Mama?" Laura echoed.

"Girls," Aunt Minnie began, and then paused for a minute. "Your mother's not well."

The girls felt relieved. They knew that Mama sometimes caught a cold or the grippe, and that when she did, she would stay in bed for a day or two while some neighbor or relative came and helped out.

"Is she in bed?" Laura asked.

"Well," Aunt Minnie started again, "it's not that kind of sickness." Laura started for Mama's bedroom. "No, darling, she's not there," Aunt Minnie said quickly. She put her arms around Laura and kissed her. "You're a big girl, Laura. You have to set an example for Amy."

Laura began crying. "Where's my mama?" she said. "Where is she?"

"Your mother's in the hospital," Aunt Minnie said softly. "She was doing her shopping this afternoon, and she was crossing the street when a car came around the corner and skidded on the ice. Your mother tried to run, but she slipped on the ice and fell, and the car . . . Well, now don't cry, she's going to be all right." Aunt Minnie spoke very quickly now. "She'll be fine in a little while. Amy, stop crying like that. She'll be home before you know it. Your father's at the hospital with her now, and you'll see, he'll be home right away, and he'll tell you . . ."

"I want to see my mama," Laura cried.

"You will, you will," Aunt Minnie said. "Now come on, drink your cocoa. Look what I bought for you, chocolate marshmallow cakes."

Laura said she didn't want anything and ran crying into their bedroom. But Amy sat down at the table and began eating. She was still crying a little, and the cocoa felt snug and warm in her stomach. Laura's crying had upset her the most. Mama had always been there as long as she could remember, and she knew that Mama always would be there. She would be home soon, by tonight at the very latest, and everything would go on in the same way.

After she finished her cocoa and cake, Aunt Minnie kissed her again and said she was a good girl. She gave her the other cake, Laura's cake, and Amy ate that too.

"When's Daddy coming home?" Amy asked.

"I don't know," answered Aunt Minnie. "But why don't you go outside and play?"

Amy walked into the bedroom where Laura lay stretched out across the bed, crying.

"Don't cry, Laura," she said, "Mama's going to be all right."

"Go away," Laura mumbled.

Amy shifted around uncomfortably. She wondered if she should join Laura on the bed and cry with her, but she really didn't feel there was anything to worry about. She touched Laura's arm hesitantly and said, "Come on outside and play. Everything's all right."

"Oh, go away," Laura said roughly, and pushed her arm.

"O.K., if you feel like that," Amy said in a very hurt way. She hurried into her outdoor clothes and marched stiffly out of the room to the door. But as she stood there with her hand on the doorknob, she wondered if she should leave Laura like that. Of course Laura had snapped at her and pushed her, but how could she just go away and forget all about her lying there and crying?

She walked slowly back to the room and said softly, "Laura, please, Laura . . ."

Laura sat up on the bed and pulled Amy down. She put her arms around her younger sister and sobbed, "I'm sorry I was so mean, but I'm worried about Mama."

"There's nothing to be worried about," Amy said confidently. "You heard what Aunt Minnie said. You'll see, Mama will be home tonight."

Laura just shook her head. "Are you going out now?" she asked.

"Yes. You come too."

"I don't feel like it," Laura said.

"Do you want me to stay here with you?" asked Amy.

Laura looked at her sister's downcast face and said, "No, you go on out. I want to read."

"All right," Amy said happily, "I'll see you later."

Outside, the warfare had commenced. No figure, whether man, woman, child, or animal, could walk safely down the block and pretend to be a neutral. Flying snowballs filled the air, and the cries of the wounded could be heard everywhere. Almost before Amy stepped from the door a snowball whizzed by her ear, and a luckier one connected with her shoulder. This was no time to be an observer, and she looked eagerly around her for a haven.

"Hey, Amy, over here," she heard, and saw Cynthia and Annette beckoning to her from behind their fortress. As she ran toward her friends, she provided a moving target for the enemy who fired away mercilessly at her from behind their encampments.

"Hurry up," ordered Cynthia, as soon as she had ducked down behind the protecting wall, "make some snowballs. We're growing short of ammunition."

They worked quickly, shaping the snow into hard round balls. From time to time Cynthia would stand up, shout "Ha, ha, ha," and duck down quickly as dozens of snowballs came flying over the wall. The girls caught as many of these as they could and added them to their pile. They took their hats off and raised them on their hands over the top of the walls, as decoys. The answering rain of snowballs provided them with an additional supply of ammunition, but it didn't last long. Throughout the whole afternoon, the girls managed to keep their fort from being captured. Once a surprise rear attack caught them a little off guard, but quickly they rallied and drove the enemy off.

The battle still raged as darkness settled on the block. No power in this world, it seemed, could persuade the determined warriors to abandon their posts. But then, almost at the same time, windows opened and mothers' voices called out: "Marcia," "Frances," "Joey," "Morris" — "Come in and eat supper."

In vain did the warriors protest: "Oh please, Ma," or "I'm not hungry," or "Just a little while longer." An armistice was declared. No Man's Land grew peaceful as one by one the weary soldiers trooped off to their houses.

Amy could hear someone bustling around in the kitchen as she stepped through the door.

"Mama?" she called.

Aunt Minnie's voice answered her. "What do you want, Amy?"

"Oh, nothing," she answered. She had almost forgotten about Mama outside, and now that it all came back to her, a strange feeling began developing inside her stomach. She walked into the bedroom and found Laura still sitting on the bed reading her book, *The Slipper Point Mystery*, by Augusta Huiell Seaman. Her face was red and puffy.

"Where's Daddy?" Amy asked.

"He's not here yet," answered Laura.

Amy wandered into the kitchen where Aunt Minnie stirred a large pot of split-pea soup.

"You can set the table, Amy," she said. "I don't think we'll wait for your father. He might be home late."

Amy brought the dishes to the table. She put her own soup bowl down at her place. It had a daisy pattern in the center, so that she had to finish whatever filled up the bowl before she could see it. Then she placed Laura's bowl with the Pinocchio in it, then Mama's bowl. . . . The outside door opened, and Aunt Minnie hurried out of the kitchen to speak to Daddy. Amy followed her, and Laura ran out of the bedroom.

"Oh, Minnie," Daddy said, and he didn't even seem to see Amy and Laura, "she's still unconscious."

"Harry," Aunt Minnie said, "shh, the children!"

Amy and Laura began crying, and then Daddy put his arms around them both and hugged them much tighter than he usually did.

"It's all right," he said, "don't worry, she'll be all right. She's hurt very bad, but don't worry, she's going to be fine."

Daddy stayed just long enough to eat his supper. Then he went back to the hospital, promising to return as soon as he could. The girls waited for him until ten o'clock, when Aunt Minnie told them to go to bed.

They lay in the dark room, and Laura said she would wait up for Daddy. Amy said she would too, but before they knew it they both fell asleep. Amy woke up very late in the night. All was very quiet, but a light came from her parents' bedroom, and she could hear someone rustling around.

"They're up late," she thought sleepily, and fell back to sleep again.

She awoke again later. The dawn was beginning to break, and she could just make out the outline of Laura's face on the pillow next to her. The light still shone in her parents' bedroom, and that unfamiliar sight at this time made her remember again what had happened.

But perhaps Mama had come home in the night, Amy thought. Perhaps she was there, and that was why the light was on. She crept out of bed and, shivering, ran barefoot into the other room. It would be good to feel Mama's warm arms around her again.

Daddy lay stretched out on the bed, sleeping, but fully dressed. His newspaper had fallen to the floor. There was no one else in the room.

Amy cried for a long time, even after Laura and Aunt Minnie came running into the room, and Daddy picked her up in his arms and told her it was all right, everything was all right.

Aunt Minnie and That Dog

Mama was getting better! Daddy said so when he came home from the hospital on the following night. The family sat around the supper table, chattering and laughing. Such a long, silent time had passed since the accident that now it seemed as if they could never say enough to one another to make up for all the unspoken words.

"When is she coming home?" Amy asked impatiently.

Daddy explained that she would have to remain in the hospital for a long time, but when he saw the gloom settling on his daughters' faces, he added gaily, "When she does come home, we'll plan the biggest party we've ever had."

The girls brightened up again. They spoke about the balloons, the ice cream, and all the fine presents they would buy. They could almost see the surprise and pleasure on Mama's face when she stepped through the door and saw the fancy decorations hanging in each room and the magnificent presents spread out before her.

But in the meantime, Daddy said, they would have to be very patient. They listened indignantly while he told them about the hospital's regulation which made it impossible for children to visit patients. They protested and complained, until Daddy said finally that he could do absolutely nothing about it, but why didn't they write to Mama and let him act as their messenger.

Every day after that Amy and Laura wrote letters to Mama, and Daddy delivered them. Sometimes they sent her funny drawings, and Laura began knitting a soft pink scarf for Mama to wear around her shoulders. They waited impatiently for Daddy every night when he returned from the hospital to hear how Mama felt, if she liked their letters, and what messages she had sent them in return.

Mama never forgot to send a message through Daddy. Sometimes she said how much she laughed over their drawings, or how much she missed them, and sometimes she said she hoped they would be good girls and "listen" to Aunt Minnie.

For Aunt Minnie had moved in with them

to stay until Mama came home again. The small dark room at the end of the hall which Mama used as a combination sewing room, guest room, and also a place to store things that didn't fit anywhere else was converted into a bedroom for Aunt Minnie.

A little nervously the girls watched the moving operation. As far as they were concerned, Aunt Minnie was hardly their favorite aunt. In the past, they had visited her on a respectable number of Sundays during the year, and had been visited in turn by her. Those visits never stood out in their minds as anything special. She had no children for them to play with, and she always seemed more interested in talking to grownups than to themselves. On their birthdays she usually gave them presents that delighted Mama and disgusted them. The presents came in plain white boxes and consisted of underwear, scarves, stockings, or some other practical item. She was old too, even older than Daddy. Although the smooth white skin on her face showed no wrinkles, her hair was completely gray. All in all, the girls had their doubts.

In the days that followed, Amy and Laura discovered first with horror, and then with surprise, how very great indeed was the difference between Mama and Aunt Minnie. Mama seldom lost her temper, but Aunt

Minnie, who appeared a perfect lady to outsiders, seemed to have a barrel of dynamite concealed somewhere about her. She exploded easily, and her shrill voice echoed throughout the whole apartment. But she never stayed angry long. One moment she might yell at Amy for putting her feet up on the bedspread, and the very next moment she might give her a penny for candy.

Aunt Minnie prided herself on her housekeeping, and it seemed to the girls that never before had their blouses crackled so stiffly with starch, or their shoes gleamed so hideously. Every morning a tornado hit the apartment, with Aunt Minnie flying from room to room, an old stocking on her head, beating, pounding, scrubbing, scolding, until amazingly enough the storm suddenly subsided and everything returned to its place, shining with uncomfortable cleanliness. Aunt Minnie had no patience with the slow, fumbling manner in which the girls went about their accustomed housecleaning duties. They found themselves suddenly freed from most chores, and they decided that after all Aunt Minnie did have a few good qualities about her.

They discovered that whereas when Mama said no, she meant no, when Aunt Minnie said no it might sometimes mean no, or it might mean maybe, or perhaps it might even mean yes. Amy found herself very good at turning a no into a yes. Aunt Minnie liked hearing nice things about herself. If someone told her that she had pretty legs or fine skin or bright blue eyes, she melted quickly. Amy made sure to tell her. This made Aunt Minnie just a little more partial to Amy than to Laura. For Laura was like Mama; she seldom said things that weren't true. Without Mama around, Amy felt much more comfortable telling lies. Sometimes Laura took it upon herself to lecture her younger sister, but this criticism hardly touched Amy. Why should she worry about what Laura said when Daddy and Aunt Minnie thought she was so cute? Sometimes though, she thought uncomfortably about Mama lying there in the hospital, and she almost felt that Mama could hear everything she said.

"But Mama wants me to be nice to Aunt Minnie," Amy tried hard to believe, and she pushed the troublesome thought from her mind.

Aunt Minnie had one weakness, however, which both girls agreed was not good. And that concerned her attitude toward animals, particularly dogs. If a cat approached Aunt Minnie while she walked along the street, she would mutter a little and step cautiously to one side until the danger had passed. But if a dog, even if it were a cunning little puppy, ambled up to her, she would immediately fly in the other direction, or remain frozen in terror to the spot until someone removed the dog.

One cold evening in late December, Daddy, Aunt Minnie, and Amy sat contentedly in their warm living room. Daddy worked away quietly at his desk, and Aunt Minnie victoriously mended an enormous hole in one of Amy's socks. Amy, curled up on the sofa, was reading when Laura came in from the street. She brought someone with her. He was small and white all over, except for one black eye which looked as if someone had socked him, and he had a long, wagging tail.

As soon as Aunt Minnie saw him, she cried, "Get that dog out of here!"

"Please, Aunt Minnie," Laura pleaded, "I found him out in the park without a collar on. He must have gotten lost, and it's so cold outside. He'll freeze to death if I put him out."

"I don't care," shrieked Aunt Minnie, her voice rising higher and higher. "Get him out of here!"

Laura saw that there would be no bargaining with her aunt, so she turned to Daddy and said, "Please, Daddy, it's so cold."

Daddy seemed embarrassed. He liked dogs a lot, and he had been looking happily at the dog, but now he turned toward Aunt Minnie, and he didn't look so happy.

"Minnie . . ." he began.

"Either that dog goes, or I go!" shouted Aunt Minnie, drawing her feet up on the couch, for the dog began nosing around, evidently deligned at meeting a whole new bunch of friends.

"Minnie . . ." Daddy started again.

"You know what dogs do to a house," roared Aunt Minnie.

"Minnie . . ." Daddy said, and stopped. But Aunt Minnie did not interrupt him this time, so he continued quickly. "You're right, an apartment is no place for a dog. But let him stay here tonight. It's too cold outside. Tomorrow, first thing, I'll call the A.S.P.C.A."

"Please, Aunt Minnie," begged the girls.

Aunt Minnie wavered. She glanced toward the dog, and the girls crossed their fingers hopefully. The dog was acting like a gentleman now, as if he understood that Aunt Minnie's decision depended upon his behavior. Modestly he sat down between the legs of the radio cabinet, his tail still wagging.

"Well, all right," snapped Aunt Minnie, "I suppose even I wouldn't turn a dog out in this weather. But you'll have to keep him out of my way tonight."

"Oh, yes, we will," said Laura, and she picked up the dog, carried him into their bedroom, and closed the door.

"I don't want him in your room when you're sleeping, though," ordered Aunt Minnie. "You can put him in the kitchen later, and make sure to close the door. Now we'll have supper."

The girls played with the dog all evening. They found that he answered to the name of Skippy, and whenever they called him he jumped up on them and licked their faces affectionately. Right after supper Aunt Minnie locked herself in her room, and stubbornly refused to come out. From time to time she opened her door and shouted down the long hall, "First thing in the morning, that dog goes!"

When the time came for Laura and Amy to go to bed, Daddy came into their room and picked Skippy up.

"I'll put him in the kitchen," he said.

The girls lay in bed, discussing the situation. "Gee, she's mean," Amy whispered.

Suddenly they heard what seemed to be laughter, coming all the way from the kitchen. They sat up in bed and heard it again, Daddy's laughter. A few moments passed while the girls waited impatiently. Finally, hurried footsteps sounded in the long hall, and then Daddy came rushing into their room, holding Skippy in his arms. A wide grin spread all over Daddy's face.

"This is the smartest dog I ever saw," he said, patting Skippy's head. Skippy licked his face in return, and Daddy hugged him. "Do you know what he just did?"

"What?" cried the girls, ready to believe that he had driven off a band of robbers or rescued Aunt Minnie from her burning bedroom.

"I brought him into the kitchen, and while I was fixing a box for him to sleep in I began whistling 'Yankee Doodle.' Well, suddenly I turned around and Skippy was up on his hind legs, dancing. I never saw anything like it. Wait, I'll show you."

Daddy put Skippy down on the floor and began to whistle "Yankee Doodle." The dog's ears rose, his tail began wagging furiously; then up he stood on his hind legs, and with his paws stretched out delicately in front of him, he danced with dainty little mincing steps.

Amy and Laura laughed and laughed until their stomachs ached.

"Wait, wait! That's not all," said Daddy. "I figured if he could do this, he could probably do other things too. Someone must have taught him lots of tricks. Look at this." Daddy bent down and said, "Shake, Skippy!" and Skippy gave Daddy his paw. They all laughed, Daddy the loudest. He was very excited, and he said, "Wait! You'll see some more. Watch this! Dead dog!" Daddy ordered, and Skippy fell on his back with his paws held pitifully up in the air.

They were still laughing when they heard Aunt Minnie's voice echoing down the hall.

"First thing in the morning, that dog goes."

Daddy stopped laughing. He picked Skippy up, and whispered, "Well, go to sleep now. I'll let him sleep in my room tonight. He might be lonesome in the kitchen."

Amy and Laura hugged one another and giggled. They had a feeling that Skippy was there to stay.

And it certainly seemed that way for a while. The following morning, Daddy and Aunt Minnie went into Aunt Minnie's bedroom and closed the door. The girls could hear the voices growing higher and higher, for Daddy's temper sometimes resembled Aunt Minnie's.

"This is no ordinary dog," Daddy shouted.

"I'm no ordinary dog, either," shouted Aunt Minnie, "and I won't be treated like one."

But Daddy finally won out. The girls promised that they would take complete charge of the dog. They would bathe him, feed him, take him out, and above all, keep him away from Aunt Minnie.

Amy's letter to Mama that night reported the good news.

December 30

Dearest Mama,

How are you feeling? I am feeling fine. When are you coming home? I have a big surprise for you, but I hope you will read my letter first and not Laura's, otherwise it will not be a surprise. We have a dog. His name is Skippy and Laura found him in the park. Ask Daddy to tell you how smart he is. Aunt Minnie is fine. We are taking good care of her like you said.

Love and x x x x x x x x,
Amy

But Skippy's own talents finally brought about his downfall. Among his other abilities, Skippy was a watchdog, the best in the world, according to Daddy and the girls. He stalked around the hall door if he heard footsteps outside, and long before a visitor knocked or rang the bell, Skippy barked. He never tried to bite anyone, though, for as soon as the visitor came through the door and was greeted by the family, his tail wagged a welcome.

"It makes you feel good to have a watchdog in the house," Laura once confided to Aunt Minnie. "No one will ever be able to rob us."

"With all the millions we've got here," snapped Aunt Minnie, "no one would want to anyway."

Aunt Minnie walked around the house looking pretty grim in the weeks that followed. She kept as far away from Skippy as she could, and always called him "That Dog." Skippy, for his part, ignored her, and it seemed as if all would work out beautifully.

Unfortunately, however, Aunt Minnie had many friends and relatives whom she liked to visit. This meant that often she would return home late at night when everyone else was asleep. As she stood outside the door, she would hear Skippy's bark, and it took a few minutes before her shaking fingers were able to put the key into the lock. Of course, once she entered the house and Skippy recognized her, he just went off without bothering her. Nevertheless, his barking frightened her so much that she said it took ten years off her life each time it happened. To avoid this, Aunt

Minnie went out less often, which certainly did not make her any more kindly disposed toward "That Dog."

One night when she came home rather late, an idea began to form in her mind. She developed a plan for fooling Skippy. What she would do, she decided, was to tiptoe up to the door, turn the key in the lock as quietly as she could, and then silently creep into the house. In this way, she thought, "That Dog" would not hear her, and therefore would not bark. Congratulating herself, she crept very quietly to the door and listened. She thought she heard a low growl on the other side of the door. She listened again and heard nothing, so happily she slipped her key gently into the lock and waited. All remained silent. Slowly she turned the key in the lock, removed it, and listened again. Not a murmur! Delighted with her brilliant plan, she carefully opened the door and began to tiptoe into the apartment.

Like a thunderbolt, a white body flew out at her, and the low growl grew into a fierce snarl. Screaming with horror, Aunt Minnie dashed back into the hall, howling, "Help, help!" at the top of her lungs. Daddy, Amy, and Laura leaped out of their beds, ran into the hall, and found Aunt Minnie fluttering and shaking like a clothesline. Wagging his tail merrily, Skippy sat a short distance away.

"What's wrong? What happened?" called the neighbors, all the way up to the fifth floor.

Daddy understood the situation immediately. "It's all right. Thanks very much. She was just frightened a little. Come inside, Minnie," he said in a low voice.

"I'll never come in again," shouted Aunt Minnie.

The neighbors, sensing the beginning of a family squabble, delicately returned to their apartments, but many doors remained open just a crack.

"Come inside, Minnie," Daddy said. "We'll talk about it inside."

"It's me or that dog," screamed Aunt Minnie. "You can take your choice."

"All right, Minnie," Daddy said wearily, "I guess you're right. Come in. The dog goes tomorrow."

"He tried to bite me," Aunt Minnie said shuddering.

"Well, what do you expect if you come sneaking in like that?" Laura said. "He thought you were a robber."

"That's enough, Laura," Daddy said severely. "Go back to bed, both of you, and take Skippy in with you. He can sleep in your room tonight."

Daddy pulled Aunt Minnie into the house, and after placing her in her room, he came into the girls' room and said gently, "Your aunt is right. This is no place for a dog." He looked at Amy's and Laura's sour faces. "After all," he laughed, "if it's a choice between Aunt Minnie and Skippy, we certainly want Aunt Minnie to stay."

He paused, but seeing that the girls did not seem convinced, went on quickly, "Besides, it'll be better for Skippy to have companionship. Mrs. Kaplan once offered to take him. She thinks he's a wonderful dog, and I'm sure she'll take good care of him. He'll be able to play with her dog, Spotty, and you know Mrs. Kaplan will always be happy to have you visit him whenever you want."

"It's not the same," Amy said.

Daddy kissed them both. "There's no point in talking about it any more. I was wrong to let him stay when I knew your aunt was so afraid of dogs. But someday we'll get a dog. You'll see."

Next morning, Daddy took Skippy away. Amy and Laura didn't talk to Aunt Minnie for four days, even though she baked them a chocolate cake and took them to the movies in the middle of the week.

More Pets

A few weeks after Skippy's departure, Daddy
came home with something inside of his coat.

"Minnie . . . ." he said.

Aunt Minnie raised her head and looked at
that moment like a big bloodhound who could
smell danger in the air.

"Mr. Russo, the druggist, has a cat; and his
cat had kittens a few weeks ago. I was just
in there, and I thought that the girls . . ."

"Harry," interrupted Aunt Minnie, "I will
not have a cat in this house."

Through the opening in Daddy's coat a
slight movement could be seen. The girls
watched it, fascinated. Soon another movement followed, and after that a little yellow
and white striped head appeared, and a pair
of blue eyes gazed pitifully around. Amy and
Laura shrieked with delight.

It took a whole evening of sighs, tears, and
promises to persuade Aunt Minnie to change

her no to a yes. Perhaps she still felt a little sorry about Skippy, because she finally did agree.

The girls named the kitten Herky. For the first few nights, his cries and moans kept the whole family awake, and Aunt Minnie entertained them during the days with information she gathered on disposing of unwanted cats. Finally the kitten settled down, the nights grew peaceful, and again it seemed as if this pet was here to stay.

The girls loved Herky wholeheartedly, and he for his part tolerated them. But he adored Aunt Minnie. He followed her all over the house, meowing pitifully at her heels. Even her cries of "Skat" or "Get this cat away from me" had no effect on his devotion. Just as Skippy had merely been "That Dog" to Aunt Minnie, Herky was likewise only "This Cat." She avoided him completely, and never once did a kind remark about him escape from her lips.

Herky searched out Aunt Minnie's slippers. If she ran away from him, at least her slippers did not. He would sit contentedly inside one of them until one dark morning Aunt Minnie put her foot into it and came in contact with an adoring ball of fur. Her scream brought the whole family nervously into her room, to find Aunt Minnie in a fury on the bed, and Herky on the floor, gazing at her with the greatest love and admiration.

After that, the door of her room always remained closed, but somehow or other true love will always find a way, and somehow or other Herky often managed to get in. He did things, too, in the middle of her carpet which hardly increased her affection for him. Often, while the family ate its meals, Herky would sneak under the table and try to rub his little body against her legs. This generally resulted in a frightened howl from her, and sometimes a broken dish or two.

But even a love as great as Herky's for Aunt Minnie could not withstand continued coldness. One afternoon when the girls came home from school, Herky had disappeared.

"I just left the window open for a few minutes to air out the apartment," Aunt Minnie explained with a gleam in her eye, "and the dumb cat just took a walk for himself. Don't worry, he'll be back as soon as he's hungry."

But Herky never returned. Amy and Laura felt that Aunt Minnie purposely opened the window to get rid of him, and even though she denied it, she seemed too happy to be innocent. The girls combed the neighborhood in search of Herky, but no trace of him could be found. Unhappily they came to the conclusion that Herky must have died in the cold weather, and that Aunt Minnie was a murderess.

After Herky's departure Aunt Minnie's face lost that grim look, and her temper seemed unbelievably sweet. But the girls were restless. They had come to realize the wonder of a pet in a household, and their minds worked actively.

One day Amy and Laura walked all the way to Southern Boulevard from their house. There was a large five-and-ten-cent store there, and between them they had forty cents to spend. Amy wanted to buy a new jigsaw puzzle, but Laura insisted that some modeling clay would be more fun.

As they stood there discussing the problem, Laura suddenly poked Amy and pointed to a sign hanging on one of the far off walls. BABY CHICKS FOR SALE — 20¢ EACH, read the sign. The desire for the puzzle or the modeling clay disappeared as the girls darted across the floor and stopped before the large cage holding the chicks. They cooed and clucked as the chicks strutted back and forth before their enchanted eyes. Their little yellow bodies just seemed to cry, "Take me home." They bought two of them. Laura said she thought one of them would turn into a rooster, and maybe when they grew up, they might have more baby chicks.

"We'd never sell them, would we, Laura?" asked Amy.

"Of course not. We'll keep them as pets. Maybe they'll lay eggs, and we can sell those."

All the way home, the girls discussed their plans. The saleswoman had put the chicks into a cardboard box with holes in it, and the cheeps of the little chicks came clearly through.

One thing Amy and Laura had to admit, and that was that Aunt Minnie was pretty smart, all right. She opened the door for them, looked quickly at the box, and said firmly, "I don't know what you've got in that box . . ." The cheeps of the chicks could be heard very clearly. "It sounds like chickens to me, but probably living here with you people has been driving me crazy. Anyway, whatever you've got there isn't coming into this house."

"But Aunt Minnie," said Laura shrewdly, "we'll be able to make a lot of money when they grow up and lay eggs."

"Laura," Aunt Minnie said, and her face wore that grim look again, "take those things back where you got them. Neither one of you can come into this house until you get rid of them, whatever they are."

As the girls walked back to the five-and-ten-cent store, they considered for a while running away from home and starting a chicken farm someplace. But by the time they reached the store they were so cold and tired that they just wanted to get rid of the chicks. However, the saleswoman refused to take them back. Laura spoke to the manager, but he too remained stubborn.

Back the girls trudged, feeling so miserable that they could barely talk to one another.

"What are we going to do now?" whined Amy.

"How do I know?" barked Laura.

A block away from home, they met Herbert Steinman, who was in Laura's class.

"What have you got in the box?" asked Herbert.

Laura gave Amy a look which meant "Let me do the talking." "Baby chicks," she said sweetly. "Aren't they cute?" She let Herbert look into the box.

"I'm going to be a veterinarian when I grow up," he said seriously. "I'd like to get some chicks too. Where did you buy them?"

"In the five-and-dime store on Southern Boulevard," said Laura, and Amy could see that she was trying to figure out a plan. But for Amy, it was simple.

"These were the last ones they had," she said. She looked triumphantly at Laura, and it seemed to her for the first time that her older sister approved of her lie.

"Shucks!" complained Herbert. "I really wanted them."

"Well," said Laura, turning toward Amy, "why don't we let him have them then? If he's going to be a veterinarian, he needs to be able to study animals. He'll probably know how to take better care of them than we would anyway."

Amy appeared to be considering the matter, and Herbert said anxiously, "Oh, I'd take good care of them. You could come over and play with them whenever you want, and I'll even let you take them home with you sometimes over weekends."

"Well, O.K.," said Amy slowly.

Herbert smiled and said he thought they were pretty nice for girls. "How much are they?" he asked.

"Twenty-five cents each," Amy said quickly, figuring on a small profit. But honest Laura gave her a dirty look and said nobly, "But you can have them for twenty cents each."

Herbert looked suspicious at this unwarranted generosity.

"If you promise, though," Laura continued desperately, "to give us some eggs free of charge when they begin to lay them."

"All right, I will," agreed Herbert. He dug into his pockets, but found that he had only seven cents. The girls kindly agreed that he could pay them later.

But Herbert's mother also refused to allow the chicks to come into the house, and since Amy and Laura refused to take them back, Herbert passed them on to Katherine Brady. When her mother said no, she gave them to Joan Perry. In the days that followed, the chicks were passed around a great deal, but remained amazingly healthy in spite of irregular feedings and much handling. Finally Mrs. Goldman took them. She said that she would raise them until they grew fat, and then she would eat them.

To the children in the neighborhood, she appeared like the witch in *Hansel and Gretel*, and nobody smiled at her anymore. Various plans were discussed for rescuing the chicks, but all seemed doomed to failure. Finally Laura told Miss Hilton, her teacher, the whole story, and Miss Hilton spoke to Mr. Gray, the nature teacher. He said he would keep the chicks in the nature room if the children could convince Mrs. Goldman to give them up.

Mrs. Goldman said no. Delegations of children visited her each day. They pleaded with her, bribed her, and threatened to kidnap the chicks. But Mrs. Goldman said no. She kept the chickens in her bathroom, and as the weeks passed, they grew fatter and fatter, and the children waited breathlessly for the execution.

But events took a surprise turn.

February 27

Dearest Mama,

How are you feeling? I am feeling fine. Mrs. Goldman is a very nice lady. I like her and so does Laura. Yesterday she told us that she is not going to kill the chickens. She said she is used to them now and they are like her own family. They keep her company, she says. She does not mind a little dirt. Aunt Minnie says she is crazy and that she must be the only person in the whole Bronx who has chickens. When are you coming home?

Love and x x x x x x x x,
Amy

When spring came, Amy and Laura's restlessness began again. One day, as they walked through the park, they noticed the caterpillars winding along the ground, their yellow and black bodies brilliant in the sunshine.

"Gee, they're pretty," Amy said wistfully.

"They turn into butterflies," said Laura, and she and Amy looked quickly at one another. They pulled a box out of one of the garbage cans and filled it with grass. Then they collected about thirteen caterpillars and placed them carefully into the box. Aunt Minnie, luckily, was out shopping when they returned home, and they smuggled the box into their bedroom.

Surprisingly enough, Aunt Minnie did not object too strenuously to the caterpillars as long as they stayed inside the box. Every day Amy and Laura would peer hopefully into the box to see whether or not the caterpillars had changed into butterflies.

"I think that one over there is changing," Laura might whisper. Or Amy might say, "I think that little one is beginning to sprout wings."

But the days passed, and no butterflies appeared. However, the caterpillars managed, somehow or other, to crawl out of the box. Laura and Amy could only remember bringing home thirteen caterpillars, but they had to admit that either those thirteen certainly got around fast, or another fifty had been hidden in the grass.

Aunt Minnie's temper did not improve on finding caterpillars lolling along on her pillow, nestling among the silverware, or winding gracefully along under the sink. Martial law was declared, and the house was turned upside down until Aunt Minnie had flushed the last caterpillar down the toilet.

Amy and Laura went on a hunger strike for two meals. But with the appearance of chocolate pudding and whipped cream at the supper table, they surrendered temporarily and decided to change their tactics.

The next day, right after school, they packed a few of their cherished belongings and announced to Aunt Minnie that they were leaving home.

"Fine," said Aunt Minnie, "but be home in time for supper."

Heads held high, they marched out of the house and walked over to Grandma's. They told Grandma the whole sad story, but she just gave them some honey cake and milk, a long lecture about behaving themselves and being grateful to Aunt Minnie, and shipped them off home again.

Daddy met them on their arrival home, and they had to listen to another lecture about ingratitude and lack of respect. Daddy also informed them that he intended to suspend their allowances for a week.

As they lay in bed that night, discussing the situation, Aunt Minnie figured largely in their conversation. They said she was a cruel, spiteful person who hated children, and that they would be glad when she left them. They also wondered how much a monkey cost.

A few days later, when they returned from

school, they found a round package, covered with brown paper sitting on the kitchen table. It did not have the look of an ordinary shopping bundle, and they glanced wonderingly at Aunt Minnie.

She had a happy look on her face, and she said, "It's a present for you two. I don't want you to think your nasty, old Aunt Minnie doesn't love you."

Eagerly the girls removed the paper. A round glass globe appeared which contained two bright orange fish, swimming gracefully above colored pebbles.

"Goldfish!" cried Amy.

"My favorite fish!" yelled Laura.

They ran to Aunt Minnie and hugged her.

"They're really very nice pets," Aunt Minnie said happily, "beautiful, too. And besides," she sighed contentedly, "they can't get out."

Rosa

"You disgust me!" Laura suddenly said to Amy, and quickly walked away.

"What's biting her?" asked Cynthia, very surprised.

"Oh, who knows?" Amy tried to keep her voice from trembling, but the big bubble of shame that had been steadily growing inside her rose up, and she felt her face grow hot and moist. "She's always picking on me."

The girls were walking home from school. They continued for a while in silence, and then Cynthia began talking about Rosa again. From time to time Amy nodded and joined in, but she hardly heard what her friend was saying.

"Who cares about Rosa anyway?" she thought angrily to herself. "And why does Laura always have to be around when I don't want her?" But she knew that Laura would be waiting for her at home, and she also knew that there was absolutely nothing she could say in her own defense.

It had all started yesterday. In the morning Miss Parker, Amy's 5A teacher, had marched the class downstairs to the yard for recess and informed them that the girls would jump rope and the boys would play punch ball. Cynthia and one or two other girls who preferred punch ball to rope squirmed unhappily in their places, but no disapproving voices were raised. They all knew by this time that Miss Parker was a lady who did not apreciate differences of opinion. Quietly they lined up under her direction, the enders began turning the rope, and Miss Parker moved off to organize the boys.

Miss Parker waddled when she walked. She was a large woman and very imposing from the front. It was only when she turned her back and began walking that the children could dare to notice her resemblance to a rather big duck. As soon as she was at a safe distance a few low giggles broke from the line of girls. Amy stood close to the front of the line. In front of her was Rosa, and in front of Rosa, Annette DeLuca.

Some louder giggles from behind her made Amy turn her head. She saw Cynthia, who usually stood at the end of the line out of her place, waddling up and down and flapping her hands. Of course, she was careful to walk on the side of the line away from Miss Parker's vision, and the girls, who all started laughing, were careful to keep their laughter low. Amy laughed especially hard. Cynthia was so wonderful! She could mimic anybody, and she was so brave, Amy thought. Nobody else would dare to imitate Miss Parker right under her nose. Cynthia continued waddling up and down the line until finally the laughter petered out and somebody said, "Well, let's start the game."

Most of the girls looked away from Cynthia to the enders, who began turning once more. Cynthia continued flapping her hands a few more times, but when she saw that hardly anyone besides Amy was watching she stopped; but a big smile was still spread across her face. The first girl began jumping, and Cynthia watched her for a moment. Then she turned slowly and seemed to be on her way back to the end of the line.

Suddenly she changed her mind and announced, still smiling, "I don't like it back there."

She shoved herself into the line right behind Annette, flapped her hands a few more times, and said "Quack."

Rosa, caught off balance when Cynthia pushed into the line, fell back, stepping hard on Amy's foot.

"Ouch!" yelled Amy, but she was still laughing.

"Oh, I am sorry," said Rosa, and then turning to Cynthia, she said, "That is not your place."

"Says who?" grinned Cynthia.

"I say so," Rosa answered in a voice that was low but annoyed.

Cynthia turned completely around and looked wonderingly at Rosa.

"Well, it's my place now," she said slowly and clenched her fists, "unless you want to do something about it."

Rosa began to laugh. "I will not fight for a small thing like that," she said. "You may stay where you are."

It all happened so quickly and so quietly that only Amy heard the whole thing.

"She sounded just like a grownup talking to a child," she told Laura later that day, "and I could tell she wasn't afraid of Cynthia at all."

"Well, it's about time," said Laura, "that somebody put that little bully in her place. The rest of you are all scared stiff of her. But what's this Rosa like anyway?"

So Amy began to tell Laura about Rosa.

She told her about Rosa's beautiful long, black braids and her serious face. She told her how hard Rosa worked to learn English and how much her speech had improved. And she told Laura what the girls thought of Rosa.

"They think she's stuck up, and they make fun of her behind her back, especially Cynthia. But Cynthia's wrong. She's not really stuck up, just shy. She'd love to play, but they never ask her and she's not the kind of girl to run after anybody. I guess she's proud."

Laura nodded. "Why don't you ask her to play?" she said.

Amy didn't answer.

Then Laura went on. "There's a girl in my class. Her name is Julia Ramon. Maybe she's been in this country a year or so. She's always laughing — whatever anybody says to her, she laughs." She thought a moment. "I guess she wants everybody to like her."

"Do they?" Amy asked.

"Oh, I don't know. They don't care that much about her, but nobody picks on her the way they do with Rosa. But I'll tell you one thing," Laura said very seriously, "if Rosa was in my class, I wouldn't just stand around and let the other kids pick on her. I'd do something."

Amy knew Laura would do something, and she felt proud of Laura. Laura was brave.

Rosa was brave too, she guessed, and she admired bravery more than anything else. Poor Julia Ramon! Amy had the unhappy feeling that if she, Amy, were to move to a different country, she might also act just like Julia Ramon.

"I always thought Rosa was a nice girl," she told Laura, "and I always felt bad when the other kids laughed at her, but what can I do? I'm new here too."

Laura didn't say anything.

After a while Amy went on: "Maybe tomorrow I'll talk to her. Maybe she'd like to come over some afternoon. I'll ask her tomorrow."

And Laura smiled at her and nodded.

"Sure," she said. "Why not?"

"Why not?" Amy kept saying to herself the next day at school. She had a happy, trembly feeling inside her as she watched Rosa. Every so often she would catch Rosa's eye and smile, and Rosa always smiled back.

"As soon as I get a chance," Amy thought, "I'll talk to her. When nobody else is around..."

In the course of the morning, Miss Parker announced to the class that she had something special to tell them.

"Class 8B," she said, "is preparing to give

a spring play for the school, and they've asked for our help."

The children were suspicious. They could think of no possible reason in the world why the mighty 8B class should need their help or anybody else's help for that matter.

Miss Parker explained that many of the parts in the play were flower parts. One child would be the rose, another the daisy, and so on. But there was one part that needed a younger, smaller child, and that was the violet. Naturally, said Miss Parker, class 8B didn't want a child from the lowest grades because a very young child couldn't be expected to learn the lines properly.

The children waited eagerly for what was coming.

But, said Miss Parker, a child from 5A was old enough to understand the lines and follow direction. The child who was selected would, of course, have to study the lines at home, and would receive special permission to practice with 8B for at least one period every day. Now, said Miss Parker, was there any girl in the class who would like to try out for the part?

Every girl in the class raised her hand.

Miss Parker smiled. "I'm afraid it will have to be somebody rather small," she said.

A few of the girls lowered their hands, but the air was still filled by many waving, pleading hands.

"Now let me see," Miss Parker mused. Her eyes skimmed rapidly over the beseeching faces. Amy wiggled her hand as hard as she could, and her face assumed her most winning smile. Miss Parker smiled encouragingly at her, but her eyes continued moving over the faces.

"Annette DeLuca, you may come up here. Bernice ... Helen ... and ..." It was a long moment as Miss Parker took one last look around the room. "Rosa Ferrara," she said.

The girls who were selected moved quickly up to the front of the room. It just wasn't fair, Amy grumbled to herself. After all, she was one of the smallest girls in the class — certainly Bernice and Helen were taller — and she just knew that she could be a perfect violet. But that's the way it always was.

She looked enviously at the four girls in the front of the room. Annette had all the luck. Teachers always liked her. Then Amy became aware of Rosa standing there too. Rosa's eyes were shining, and she was trying hard not to smile.

"I'm glad Miss Parker picked her," Amy thought, forgetting all about herself, "but I guess she doesn't have much of a chance."

Miss Parker handed Annette a slip of paper and told her to read it out loud to the class. It contained some of the lines that the violet would speak in the play.

Annette smiled and began reading. Her voice was clear, and she spoke very distinctly. When she had finished, Miss Parker nodded approvingly and handed the slip to Bernice.

Bernice was nervous. Her hand shook, rattling the paper, and her voice squeaked. Although Amy was sympathetic, she had to admit that Annette had been much better.

Now it was Rosa's turn. Rosa began reading so softly that nobody could hear her, and Miss Parker interrupted and told her to start over again, and louder this time. Rosa nodded, wrinkled her forehead a little, and began again. This time everybody could hear her, and understand her too. The words sounded a little furry, but quite clear. Rosa's voice was soft and very sweet, and she spoke the lines as if she liked them.

"Why, she's even better than Annette," Amy thought in surprise and delight.

"That was very good," said Miss Parker.

She handed the paper to Helen, who read the lines in a loud, cheerful voice.

"Well," said Miss Parker when Helen had finished, "you were all very good. It's not going to be easy making a decision. I had no idea we had so many stars in this class."

The four girls smiled because it was expected of them, but their hearts were pounding and they could hardly wait for Miss Parker to announce her decision.

"I do think, though," Miss Parker finally said, "that since the violet is such a modest, gentle flower, Rosa probably would do best in the part. Her voice is so soft and violety."

She smiled kindly at Annette, Bernice, and Helen. "It's too bad they don't need any others because the three of you are so good."

Then she waved vaguely in the direction of the class, and the three girls understood that the audition was over and that they were to sit down. Hiding their disappointment behind cheerful smiles, they walked toward their seats.

Miss Parker turned and began talking to Rosa. Rosa was smiling. It was good seeing Rosa smile; and Amy smiled too, she was so happy that Rosa had been chosen. Of course Rosa certainly had spoken the lines better than anyone else. There was no question about that. She guessed that now the girls saw how good she was they would like her better and stop picking on her. Miss Parker handed Rosa a pass, and Rosa left the room. Later, when she came back, Amy would tell her how good she sounded. She could hardly wait.

Rosa was gone most of the morning. During recess, the girls gathered together and began discussing Miss Parker's choice.

"She's crazy," Cynthia said, "Annette was just wonderful. Even Bernice and Helen were better than Rosa."

Annette tossed her head and tried to look unconcerned.

"Who cares?" she said. "It was a silly part anyway. I suppose Miss Parker felt sorry for Rosa. She'll ruin the whole play. Nobody will be able to understand anything she says."

Amy looked around at the girls who stood listening. They were nodding their heads in agreement. But how could they? Amy wondered. Rosa spoke very clearly now, and all of them must know she was the best. Should she say something? She wanted to, but the girls all seemed so annoyed.

Millie Wagner began talking. She was a serious, studious girl whose mother still brought her to school in the mornings and waited to take her home in the afternoons.

"I thought Rosa was very good," she said, "and I understood every word she read."

"You must be deaf, Millie," Cynthia said, and the other girls smiled. Millie's cheeks turned pink, and she walked away.

"Takes a girl like that," said Annette, "to like Rosa."

Amy decided that she'd better not say anything, and that perhaps she should wait and congratulate Rosa tomorrow.

On the way home from school Cynthia continued talking about Rosa, even after Laura had joined them.

"She must think she's the Queen of Sheba or something, the way she always acts like she's better than we are."

She turned toward Amy.

"Ye-e-es," said Amy, and wished Laura would go away. But Laura continued walking silently along with them.

"I sure told her off yesterday while we were jumping rope. She was pretty scared too. You heard me, didn't you?" asked Cynthia.

"Ye-e-es," whispered Amy.

"Who does she think she is, anyway? It's just not fair that she got the part. All the kids wanted it, and anybody could be a better violet than she could."

Amy suddenly thought of something very funny to say. She knew Cynthia would laugh, and she couldn't help laughing herself as she said, "Rosa's no violet — she's poison ivy."

Cynthia did laugh, but it was then that

Laura said, "You disgust me!" and walked away.

Now Amy stood on her stoop outside the house and tried not to think. She laid her books on the stone ledge and wished that something would happen to stop her from thinking. Buster came bounding up the steps from the basement, barking joyfully. "He always knows when I'm here," Amy thought proudly, and walked over to where Buster's snout protruded eagerly between the familiar bars.

"Nice boy, good boy." Amy kneeled down and let Buster lick her face.

Buster stopped for a moment and looked around expectantly.

"I don't have a pretzel," Amy apologized, "but I'll buy you one later."

Buster licked her face again. She patted his head lovingly.

"At least you'll always like me," she said. "You don't think I'm so terrible."

A few more licks and then Buster lay down on the platform, his tail still thumping.

"I'll buy you a pretzel later," Amy promised again. She stood up, brushed herself off slowly, and slowly walked back to the stoop. All her unpleasant thoughts returned.

She just knew Laura would say something

about Mama. Lately, whenever they argued, Laura always managed to have the last word by saying, "How do you think Mama would feel if she knew?"

Of course, Amy realized that nobody would tell Mama anything unpleasant about her or anybody else. That didn't worry her at all. Daddy kept saying that Mama must hear only cheerful things, and that their letters to her should be happy and uncomplaining. Laura thought she didn't want Mama to know about the bad things she did, but Laura was wrong. If Mama was home now she wouldn't be standing outside thinking. She would be inside, crying in Mama's lap and telling her all about it. And Mama would scold her and tell her how shamefully she had behaved. But then Mama would end up by consoling her, because she always understood how much Amy hurt inside.

After telling Mama, Amy always felt better and always knew how she should behave until the next time. But Mama had been away in the hospital now for more than three months, and inside Amy there grew a mountain of all the bad things Mama didn't know about, and all the hurt feelings Mama hadn't kissed away.

"Mama, Mama," Amy whispered, "come

home, please. There's no more room inside me."

Tears rose to her eyes, but she forced them back. What was the point of crying? Laura waited for her inside, not Mama.

"I may as well get it over with," she decided. She straightened herself and began arranging her thoughts for the coming battle.

"I'll just tell her it's a free country and I can say what I like. Who does she think she is anyway? Cynthia's my best friend, and who cares about Rosa!"

As she picked up her books and started walking slowly toward the door, she practiced in her mind the many things she would tell Laura.

"I don't even like Rosa," she thought, trying to make her anger grow bigger than her shame, "and I don't like you either, Laura."

She walked up the steps and stood at last outside the apartment. Her hand rested on the doorknob, and she took one deep breath before turning it.

"And I don't like myself," said something else deep inside her. But angrily she dismissed that thought from the others, opened the door, and walked in.

April Fool

The sun had just risen that morning, and came through the living-room windows, filtered by the lace curtains. It cast little squares of light on the floor, on the old, faded furniture, and on the bumpy walls. Six o'clock in the morning, and the street still slept, except for the occasional, hurrying footsteps that carried the milkman and the baker home from work.

Suddenly the alarm clock in Daddy's room started ringing, loud and demanding. A sleepy arm emerged from underneath Daddy's blanket, groped around, found the clock, and turned it off. Daddy groaned sleepily and settled back to enjoy another ten or fifteen minutes of delicious half-wakefulness. A stifled giggle from the living room, and there it was again — the maddening sound of an alarm clock. Automatically Daddy's arm reached out, pressing the buzzer on his clock, once, twice, three times, but the ringing continued.

Daddy raised himself feebly on one elbow. His eyelids struggled heavily to open.

"What's happening?" he mumbled.

He glared at his clock, but even in his half-awake state he could see that this one was not guilty. The ringing went on unchecked.

"Must stop that noise," he mumbled, staggering out of bed. He slipped his right foot into his left slipper and, forgetting about the other slipper, hurried into the living room. That's where it was coming from — the electric clock on top of the radio. He turned off the alarm and leaned exhausted on the radio cabinet.

"Now how could that have happened?" he wondered drowsily. "Something must be wrong with the clock. I'll have to look into it." He glanced longingly toward his bedroom. Maybe he could just lie down for another few minutes and . . .

But there it was again — an alarm clock still ringing. Daddy shook his head back and forth a few times. Was he dreaming all this? It just couldn't be possible that every clock in the house had gone haywire. And yet it was quite clear that somewhere in the house a clock was certainly ringing. He listened intently. From the kitchen — that's where.

Daddy groped his way down the long hall, groaning every time his one bare foot touched the cold floor.

"The kitchen clock on the refrigerator," he muttered, as he reached up to turn it off. The clock was not there. But somewhere in that room a clock was ringing. After turning in all directions. Daddy finally managed to focus his eyes on a big black pot on the stove that seemed to be screaming. Impossible! But Daddy reached inside, found the runaway clock, turned it off, and stood listening, one hand in the pot. All was quiet.

"Now how could a clock get inside a pot?" Daddy said out loud, awake at last.

"April Fool!" came the answer to his question, and turning around he saw Amy, Laura, and Aunt Minnie standing in the hall, their eyes shining with pleasure.

"And it's only six o'clock," giggled Amy.

With as much dignity as he could command, Daddy removed his hand with the clock from the pot. Grimly he checked the time. Six o'clock it was, and he normally slept until seven thirty.

"That's a fine thing!" he said angrily, "Waking up a hard-working man just for a crazy joke."

There were more giggles from the three culprits.

"I don't know what's the matter with you," Daddy continued, "especially you, Minnie. It nearly scared the life out of me, and it's not a bit funny." At this point Daddy smiled a weak little smile. "Not a bit funny," he said, beginning to laugh like the rest of them. "Don't worry, I'll fix all of you for this."

Aunt Minnie wiped a tear away from one eye. "That's the best laugh I've had in ages," she said.

As the girls dressed, they discussed their plans for the day. This was their first April Fool's Day in the new neighborhood, and they had collected a number of tricks through the years that they intended trying out on their new friends. Laura had a rubber chocolate that she planned to offer David Ostrow, and Amy owned a phony inkblot that she was going to put on her teacher's desk. The night before, both girls had made little signs saying "Kick Me," and these were to be fastened on to any unsuspecting back that turned up. It promised to be a fine day.

On the way to school a number of children called out to them, "Hey, you dropped your handkerchief." But Amy and Laura did not even bother to look. That was an old, tired trick that they never used anymore. Everyone knew that one. They met Cynthia, and she taught them a new one.

"Oh, look at that big spot on your coat," she said, and put her finger on Amy's chest. As Amy bent her head down to look, Cynthia raised her finger quickly and twitted Amy's nose. "April Fool!" she shouted.

No one could sit still in his seat that morning, and yet Miss Parker seemed unaware of what today was. She told Harold Marcus twice to stop spinning around in his seat like a top, and once she announced in a loud voice to the class, "Now stop all this racket. I just don't understand what's wrong with you today."

Amy waited until the class began working on long-division problems. As Miss Parker turned her back to the class to write the problems on the blackboard, Amy poked the girl in front of her, and handed her the inkblot. Down the row it passed until Ruth Scheiner, the first girl in the row held it in her hand. Cautiously she stood up and tossed the inkblot onto the teacher's desk.

Looking as innocent as they could under the circumstances, the children pretended to be working on their problems. For the first time that morning, absolute silence filled the classroom. To Miss Parker, this was a sure danger sign, and she looked suspiciously at the children whose faces wore unusually studious expressions. She should have realized that this was too good to be true, but gratefully she sat down at her desk.

She did not see the thirty-eight pairs of eyes, seemingly intent upon arithmetic problems, peeping out at her. The eyes watched as she searched for a pencil, watched as she suddenly jumped a little in her seat. Thirty-eight pairs of ears heard her startled cry of "Oh!" and thirty-eight happy voices cried out "April Fool!"

Miss Parker looked surprised for a moment. "Oh, my," she finally said, smiling a little sadly, "I had forgotten all about it." The children chuckled.

By the afternoon, Amy had managed to pin three of her signs on three different backs, and somebody had slipped a piece of banana down the inside of her blouse. As she wiggled in her seat, trying to dislodge all the gooey pieces, she heard stifled giggles all around her. At first she thought it had to do with her, but as she listened she noted that the giggles started up suddenly, stopped for a moment, and then started up again.

Suddenly the girl behind tapped Amy's shoulder and passed her a note. Carefully she unfolded it and read:

"Look at the footprints on the ceiling."

Immediately, Amy's eyes traveled upward. She saw no footprints, but she did hear again the sound of those mysterious giggles.

At the bottom of the note it said "Pass this." Amy smiled and handed the note to the girl in front of her. When she looked up, Amy and all the other children aware of the joke giggled into their handkerchiefs. The note continued to circulate, and there were more and more giggles.

Suddenly Miss Parker leaped from her seat and grabbed the note just as Melvin Potter was passing it to Raymond Anderson.

"I'm going to put an end to all this nonsense right now," Miss Parker said sharply. "You've done nothing all day but get into trouble."

She opened the note and read it. A delicious silence attended her, but as soon as Miss Parker's eyes traveled to the ceiling, the silence was broken by the loudest laugh that had ever echoed down the halls of the school. Silence was soon restored, however, by Miss Parker's announcement that everyone in the class would be expected to hand in a special assignment the next morning. The assignment consisted of the sentence, "I will not pass notes," written one hundred times. Her threat of expanding it to two hundred times, or even five hundred if necessary, restored order for the rest of the afternoon.

When Amy and Laura arrived home from school, they found Daddy waiting for them on the stoop. Usually Daddy did not come home from work before five o'clock, and the girls were surprised to see him. The happy expression on his face reassured them that everything was all right.

"I just dropped back here for a few minutes," he explained, "Your aunt thinks I'm at work, and I'm counting on that. I thought up a wonderful joke to play on her."

The girls listened gleefully as Daddy outlined his plan. It all hinged around the telephone in the candy store. Very few people on the block owned a private phone. It was just too expensive. Whenever it became necessary to communicate with someone, a postcard or a personal visit would accomplish the business, and cost very little at the same time. However, every so often a matter might arise of such urgency that the use of a telephone became essential. In such cases the telephone in the candy store would ring, and all who heard it would realize that something unusual had happened. The person on the other end of the line would give the candy-store man the name and address of the wanted one, and a child would be sent to fetch him or her. A nickel or dime rewarded the messenger for his pains.

Daddy suggested that someone go tell Aunt Minnie there was a phone call for her. He had discussed the situation with Mr. Rosen, the candy-store man, who agreed to enter the conspiracy. In the meantime Daddy, Amy, and Laura could hide behind the candy counter in the store and watch for Aunt Minnie. At the right moment they would pop up and shout "April Fool!" Now what, Daddy asked proudly, did they think of that idea?

The girls thought the plan delightful. A boy was therefore dispatched, and the three plotters ducked behind the candy counter. After a breathless minute or two, Aunt Minnie came flying into the store, huffing and puffing. Her hair was messed up, and her old, mended stockings, the kind she wore only during housecleaning, sagged at her ankles. All in all she looked terrible, not at all the way she liked people to see her. She charged into the phone booth, picked up the receiver, and shouted, "Hello!" A second passed, and then she shouted again, impatiently, "Hello, hello!"

At that moment Daddy, Amy, and Laura came out from behind the counter, stuck their heads into the phone booth, and yelled "April

Fool!" The other people in the store who knew about the plot began laughing heartily at Aunt Minnie's dazed expression. But this time Aunt Minnie was not amused.

"You're a big baby, Harry," she said. "I got such a fright. I was up on the ladder, cleaning out the dish closet, and I nearly fell off."

The laughter of the bystanders increased, and Aunt Minnie glared at them. She cast one more angry look at Daddy, Amy, and Laura, and flounced out of the store.

Daddy treated Amy and Laura to chocolate sodas and then departed for work. The girls discussed the situation and decided, in Aunt Minnie's own words, that they had better "make themselves scarce" that afternoon. Timidly they entered the house, but Aunt Minnie and an angry lecture awaited them. She said fun was fun, and that she was the first one to laugh at a good joke. However, she said, she did not think making people fall off ladders and fracturing their skulls at all funny. As soon as they properly could, the girls disappeared. Laura hurried off to the library, and Amy went in search of Cynthia.

She found her friend in the schoolyard, and soon became involved in a game of handball. In the course of the game, Cynthia smacked the ball so hard against the wall that it went bounding furiously past Amy's outstretched hand. She chased after it, but the ball continued rolling all the way to the other end of the schoolyard and out through the open gate. The ball bounced across the street, rolled up to an iron gate that fenced off an empty lot, and disappeared inside.

A minute later Amy arrived breathlessly at the spot. While pausing to catch her breath, she studied the height of the gate. Doubtfully her eyes traveled up the high iron bars which ended in sharp points at the top. She could never climb over that gate in a million years! The best thing to do, she supposed, would be to call Cynthia. But what had happened to the ball? She could not see it anywhere.

A little farther away from where she stood, Amy suddenly noticed that two of the iron bars that formed the gate had been pushed rather widely apart. The space seemed just wide enough for a head to go through. In a moment, Amy's head was on one side of the gate while her body remained on the other. Sure enough, the ball lay just a few feet away. Well, she guessed she would go and get Cynthia. Or would she? Somehow or other, she could not pull her head back through the bars. She twisted and pulled and pushed, but her head still remained on the other side of the gate.

"What's the matter, little girl?" asked a woman's voice.

"My head," whimpered Amy, "it's stuck."

The woman grabbed Amy's shoulders and turned her body this way and that way, but in spite of all the jiggling, her head would not come out.

"What are you doing, Amy?" asked Cynthia's voice. "I didn't know what happened to you."

Amy began to cry. "I'm stuck, I'm stuck," she said. "Go get Laura and my Aunt Minnie."

She heard Cynthia's running footsteps. Soon another woman joined the first, and as they pulled and pushed her, she heard them talking about what a disgrace it was that the city left such a gate up, and about all the children who had fallen, broken arms or legs, twisted necks, cut knees and heads, and many other things.

In a little while other people joined them, and Amy could hear many voices and many sensible suggestions, but still her head stuck fast. A man suggested that someone hold her shoulders while he pick her legs up off the ground. He said if they turned her all around, maybe her head would squeeze through in another position. While she was being revolved in this fashion, she heard Cynthia's voice saying, "Gee whiz!"

"Where's Laura and my aunt?" screamed Amy.

"Gee, Amy, they wouldn't come," Cynthia said. "They didn't believe me, and they said they knew an April Fool's joke when they heard it. Your aunt even slammed the door in my face."

Amy began to howl, "I want my mama, I want my mama!"

One of the ladies patted her on the hand and said not to worry, they would get her out in no time. But moving her around off the ground did not seem to help much. Her head just became more tightly wedged between the bars, and for a while they had to hold her legs up off the ground until they could loosen her head up again.

One man, whom Amy got a glimpse of while she was being rotated, seemed to be in charge of the operation. Some of the other people seemed anxious to try other methods to free her, and she could hear the man arguing with them. Finally she stood on her feet again, in the same position that she had started from. She heard the man say angrily that it was a good thing he had come along or "they" might have broken her neck. An argument arose, and for a while nobody pushed or tugged Amy at all.

However, as soon as the fire engines were heard, the tugging and pulling began all over again. A police car soon joined the crowd, and a man with a camera climbed over the fence and started taking pictures. Amy had been crying miserably ever since the tugging had started. But at the sight of the camera, she grinned cheerfully, as she always did when someone took her picture. As soon as the photographer finished, however, she began crying again.

Judging from all the voices and noise, the crowd seemed to have grown tremendously. Two policemen tried to separate the iron bars, but they would not budge. Finally someone produced a saw, and after what seemed to to be ages, Amy found that she could stand up straight once more, turn her head from side to side, and look around her.

She saw an enormous crowd of people, all smiling happily at her. The sight of all those joyful faces just made her cry even harder than before. A pretty young woman put an arm around her and said she shouldn't cry anymore, that everything was all right now, and that she had been very brave. More people spoke to her, and even some hugged and kissed her.

She stopped crying when a man stepped forward who said he was a reporter. He asked Amy a number of questions about herself, and then he said that it would all be in the paper the next day. She started to cry again when one of the policemen spoke to her and told her never to go sticking her head where it didn't concern her. But after he had finished lecturing her, he patted her on the head and said that she had been a good girl, and she shouldn't cry anymore.

The crowd began to scatter, and Cynthia came forward and took Amy's arm.

"Gee, you're going to be in the paper," she said jealously.

Suddenly Amy felt very important. If only her family had been there to share in the glory. She rushed home as fast as she could. But nobody believed her story.

"Honestly," she said, "I got my head stuck in the fence, and the fire engines came, and I'm going to have my picture in the paper."

"Oh, sure, sure!" Laura said.

"Now stop it," barked Aunt Minnie. "Enough's enough!"

And Daddy just laughed.

But the next day, there it was on the fifth page of the newspaper. The picture showed

Amy with her head stuck between the bars, her legs held up in the air, and a gay smile on her face. Behind her, in the picture, stood all the people, looking very serious and solemn. The headline read:

CHILD'S PLIGHT MOVES HEARTS

and the article told the whole story. It also said how wonderful people are because they could drop everything and come to the aid of a child in distress. The last paragraph said that two men in the crowd were arrested for fighting, and one woman was taken to the hospital with cuts and bruises.

Laura said, "Everything nice happens to you."

But Daddy and Aunt Minnie were very proud. Aunt Minnie said that Amy was the first member of the family to have her picture in the newspaper. She bought a large number of copies and distributed them to all the important relatives and friends. Daddy took one to Mama.

"This is one April Fool you'll never forget," said Daddy to Amy.

And she never did.

The Surprise Party

April 10

Dearest Mama,

Daddy says you keep laughing every time you think about Amy's birthday. I'm glad you think it's funny, Mama, but believe me, now that the 24th is growing closer, she's become worse. Never stops talking about it. Anyway, I'm glad you like my idea. I will send you all the details. Otherwise, nothing new to tell you about. *Come home soon!* I miss you so much.

Love and x x x x x x x x,

Laura

Amy's birthday fell on April twenty-fourth. For every year, as long as she could remember, a birthday party, lasting all afternoon and evening, had marked the important event. Around two o'clock in the afternoon, the festivities generally began with a children's party. There would be presents, ice cream, coconut cake, presents, games, and presents. At five o'clock the children would go home, and shortly after that the grown-up relatives would begin to arrive. There would be more presents, more food, and much kissing and hugging of Amy. Although she always enjoyed the afternoon party the most, she had to admit that the best presents usually came in the evening. In particular, Aunt Janet, Mama's younger sister, could always be counted on for something special.

But this year, with Mama in the hospital, Amy had not thought much about a birthday party until late February. Aunt Minnie said no, which did not, of course, discourage Amy. The more she thought about it, though, the more she felt that this year she would like a different kind of party — a surprise party. She had never had one, and she decided that she wanted one. In early March, she began working at it.

"I never had a surprise party," she told Laura wistfully. "Gee, I wish someday I could have a surprise party."

"Tough!" answered Laura.

Lately Laura had developed an interest in gangster movies. As a result of this, she had picked up the word "tough," and used it whenever she could. But this did not discourage Amy.

She spoke to Aunt Minnie again in the middle of March.

"Gee, wouldn't it be wonderful to have a surprise party? I've never had one, and someday I wish I could."

Aunt Minnie just grunted and said she wished she could have a surprise party too. The best kind of surprise party for her, she said, would be if Amy hung up her clothes and washed her neck without anybody getting after her.

Things looked pretty good.

In early April, Amy saw favorable signs in the air. Whispered conversations between Aunt Minnie and Laura, which stopped suddenly whenever she entered the room, reassured her. She even heard Aunt Minnie say to Laura one day, "It's a lot of nonsense, and too much work for nothing."

Things looked pretty good indeed.

Amy wanted to have a hand in the invitations, but she realized that she would have to proceed with caution. So far, Aunt Minnie and Laura were not suspicious, and part of the fun of a surprise party lay in having people think you really did not expect one.

"You know, I like Bernice Rogers," she would announce to Laura in the days that followed, or "That Ruth Scheiner is disgusting," or "Cynthia is my best friend."

"Tough!" said Laura.

Amy wondered about Rosa Ferrara. Should she take a chance and invite her to the party? Naturally the girls wouldn't like it, but since it was a surprise party they'd assume that she had no hand in the invitations. Nobody could blame her, and she could pretend to be especially astonished when she saw Rosa. She considered the matter many times. All she'd have to do now was just mention to Laura a few times how much she liked Rosa and how she wished she knew her better. Laura would do the rest. Of course, ever since their big argument over her, Rosa's name had not been mentioned by either one of them. It would be awkward, but not impossible.

Maybe if the girls met Rosa away from school, and especially at a party where everybody was supposed to be happy and friendly, they might feel differently about her. But suppose they didn't? The whole party would be ruined. They might even suspect her of wanting Rosa to come. Then nobody would like her either. No, it wouldn't work. Probably Rosa wouldn't want to come anyway. Amy decided to forget about it.

This year April twenty-fourth fell on a Saturday, and Amy knew exactly the kind of strategy her family would use. At about ten or eleven o'clock that morning, somebody, probably Daddy or one of her friends, would take her away. This would give Aunt Minnie and Laura a chance to decorate the apartment, finish the baking, and get all the children hidden. At about two o'clock she would be brought back, and at first when she came into the house all would seem quiet. Then suddenly children would come flying from all directions, yelling "Happy Birthday," and she would have to look surprised and say something like, "What's all this?" or "Boy, is this a surprise!" She was prepared.

The first part of April went very, very slowly. On many nights Amy lay awake in bed thinking delicious thoughts, and knowing that Aunt Minnie and Laura, off in the kitchen, were discussing plans for her surprise party. She hoped they would remember to put favors in the birthday cake, and she wondered if Aunt Minnie could bake a coconut layer cake the way Mama always did. Imagine, she would be ten years old, and have *two* numbers now! Nobody could call her a baby anymore. But how strange it was to think of a birthday party without Mama. If Mama came home from the hospital on her birthday, wouldn't that really make the day complete? She thought about it, and the more she thought, the more certain she became that Mama would come home. That would be the biggest and best surprise of all.

Amy counted the days. Fifteen to go before April twenty-fourth; eleven, eight, three, and finally one morning Amy awoke and it was her birthday. She poked Laura and said, "Wake up, it's my birthday!"

Ordinarily Laura did not like to be awakened so suddenly, but today she jumped right up, yelled "Happy Birthday," and began to administer the birthday smacks. Amy ran out of the room, shrieking happily, with Laura after her.

"One, two, three," Laura yelled as she smacked her, all the way up to ten. Then she cornered Amy in the bathroom, and gave her three more smacks.

"One for good measure," Laura said, smacking lightly, "one for good luck, and one for next year," and that was the hardest smack of all.

Daddy and Aunt Minnie woke up too. They kissed Amy, wished her happy birthday, and then they all gave her their birthday presents. Amy unwrapped Laura's present first, and found the doctor's set that she had wanted for a long time. It contained a toy stethoscope, and all sorts of bandages and candy pills. She picked up Daddy's present, shook it, and pretended to wonder what it was. She unwrapped it slowly, and then cried out in delight and astonishment. "Oh, a Monopoly set! Just what I wanted." Of course she knew Daddy would buy her a Monopoly set because for the past three months she had announced to the family from time to time, "Gee, I wish I had a Monopoly set."

Aunt Minnie's present came in a square white box, and Amy held no high hopes about its contents. Sure enough, only a few pairs of long wooly underwear lay inside.

"My, isn't that nice," remarked Amy pleasantly, but not enthusiastically.

However, tucked underneath the woolies, Amy found something else which Aunt Minnie could only have purchased in a weak moment, and was sure to regret for a long time afterward. It was a pair of snow-white angora mittens, and Aunt Minnie admonished that they were only to be worn on special occasions.

Then Daddy gave Amy another package, wrapped in pretty paper and tied with a bright red ribbon. It looked like the kind of wrapping that Aunt Janet always used.

"Is this from Aunt Janet?" Amy asked, surprised.

"No. Open it and see," Daddy said, smiling.

It was a book, *Rebecca of Sunnybrook*

Farm, and when Amy opened the book she found a message written behind the title page. It said:

"To my darling Amy on her tenth birthday.

With all my love,
Mother."

"Isn't she coming home today?" Amy asked softly.

"No, darling," Daddy said. "You know, she's much better now, but it takes a long time. She didn't want you to think that she'd forgotten your birthday, so she asked Aunt Janet to buy this book for you. She said it was her favorite book when she was your age."

The family remained quiet for a moment, each one thinking the same thing.

Then Aunt Minnie said, "Well, let's have breakfast. You can choose anything you like, Amy."

"French toast," Amy ordered, "and I want real coffee."

Aunt Minnie looked grim.

"After all, I'm ten today. I'm not a baby anymore."

"All right," Aunt Minnie said firmly. "Just today, though, you can have coffee."

During breakfast, Daddy told them a story about when he and Aunt Minnie were children. There had been eight children in the family, and Amy and Laura loved to hear about their adventures. Many parents liked to tell stories about themselves when they were children, but they always sounded as if they were the kind of children who always sat quietly in their seats, always said "Please" and "Thank you," and never spoke back to grownups. But when Daddy told stories about himself or his sisters and brothers, they sounded like regular, ordinary children.

Today Daddy told them about the time a big boy started to pick on him. He was very small, and he began to cry. Who should come along at that moment but Aunt Minnie, on her way back from an errand to the grocery store. In her hand she carried a package with a herring inside it. When she saw Daddy crying and the big boy hurting him, she called out, "You stop that, you big bully!" But the boy just made a face at her and kept right on annoying Daddy. Aunt Minnie became so angry then that she took the herring and hit the boy right in the face with it.

"Of course, she ruined the herring," Daddy said sadly.

The girls giggled, and Aunt Minnie started

to say that she didn't remember ever having done such a thing in her life.

"Now, now, Minnie," Daddy said, smiling and shaking a finger at her, "nothing to be ashamed of."

Aunt Minnie smiled a little bit, then a little more. "Well," she said, "he deserved it." Soon she was giggling as much as the girls.

After breakfast, Daddy said he intended visiting Mr. and Mrs. Kaplan, and if the girls wanted to come along and play with Skippy, who lived there now, they could. Amy immediately recognized this as the signal to get her out of the house, and smiled when Laura said she was expecting her friend Marjorie Kahn, and could not go.

"Oh, sure," Amy thought to herself. "I'll come with you," she said to Daddy.

She took her pink taffeta dress out of the closet and put it on. While she was strapping on her black patent-leather shoes, Aunt Minnie came into the room and said sharply, "Now why are you wearing that? You're just going over to the Kaplans', and you'll get all messed up playing with the dog. Put your slacks on."

"Gee," Amy said wonderingly. She thought they would want her to wear party clothes.

Laura came into the room and said to Aunt Minnie, "After all, it's her birthday. She ought to wear anything she wants." Aunt Minnie looked at Laura, and Laura looked at Aunt Minnie.

"Pretty clever," Amy thought to herself, "but they can't fool little old me."

"I'll be careful," she said innocently, and Aunt Minnie answered doubtfully that she could wear anything she pleased, but she would be smart if she put her slacks on. "She sure is a good actress," Amy thought.

"Be back at two or so," Laura remarked casually, "and we'll go to the movies together."

"All right," Amy answered sweetly. She decided to tease Laura a little bit, so she added, "Maybe I ought to meet you in front of the theater." Now, how would Laura get out of that situation?

"You can if you want to," said Laura, "but I might be late, and you'd have to wait for me."

"Pretty smart," thought Amy, and she said aloud, "I'll come back and pick you up then."

Laura shrugged her shoulders.

At exactly ten minutes after two, Amy stood outside the door to the apartment, her stomach doing little, delicious flip-flops. Daddy had gone across the street to the candy store to buy some cigars, but Amy knew that this was just part of the plan. She listened, her head against the door, but all was silent inside. Of course she knew that the silence contained a dozen or so children, hidden behind doors, inside closets, under beds, giggling quietly to themselves.

Finally she rang the bell. The silence continued, and Amy could feel her heart pounding away furiously. At last the door opened, and Laura stood there with her hat and coat on.

"Let's go," said Laura.

Amy grinned a wide jack-o-lantern grin. "Just want to get something," she said, and squeezed past Laura into the house.

The apartment looked just the same as it had looked in the morning. No gay decorations hung on the walls, and no smothered giggles issued from the quiet rooms. The silence, which had seemed so full of promise just a few short moments ago, was now just silence. No question remained in Amy's mind. She had been surprised all right. There was no surprise party.

"What are you waiting for? Let's go," said Laura.

How she hated Laura, more than anyone else! Laura had led her on, had practically forced her to wear her party dress. She would get even. Her eyes began to fill with tears, and this time she did not want Laura to see her crying.

"Just a minute," she blubbered, and ran into the bathroom.

As she stood there with the tears rolling down her face, different thoughts of revenge passed through her mind. She could mess up that beautiful scrapbook that Laura was making for her history class. Maybe she should pull out all the stamps from Laura's stamp album and scatter them over the house. All the way to the movie theater, while Laura chattered on, unconscious of the plots shaping up in her sister's mind, Amy developed new ideas for revenge. Coming back from the movie, she decided that the best idea would be to take that snapshot of Laura, as a baby, stretched out absolutely naked on a bearskin, and show it to David Ostrow. He was in Laura's class, and Laura always said she hated him. Naturally, Amy figured she liked him better than any other boy.

After supper, Daddy suggested that the whole family play Monopoly with Amy's new set. Of course Laura would have to win. Every time Laura pulled in some more money, and Aunt Minnie and Daddy laughed and said she would be a millionaire when she grew up, Amy's thoughts of revenge became more elaborate and horrible.

Lying in bed that night, with Laura sleeping quietly at her side, Amy decided that no plan so far was cruel enough to properly punish her sister. But she would think of something, something really horrible.

Next morning, most of Amy's feelings of disappointment had passed away. All that remained was this question of revenge. As she sat brooding in the bedroom after breakfast, Aunt Minnie entered the room, a stocking wrapped around her head, a mop in her hand, and a determined look on her face. Today, she announced, marked the beginning of spring cleaning, and she would appreciate it very much if Amy and Laura both disappeared for a few hours. Of course, she said, if they wished to remain, she was sure she could find something for them to do.

For the moment, all thoughts of revenge vanished from Amy's mind. She hurried back into her slacks, and seeing the dainty pink party dress hanging at the front of the closet, she pushed it viciously to the back. While she was dressing, the doorbell rang and Cynthia appeared, two milk bottles in her hands.

"What's that for?" asked Amy.

"Let's go fishing," said Cynthia. "We'll go over to the park and fish in the lake."

"Are there really fish there?"

"Of course," answered Cynthia. "All we have to do is tie some string around the tops of the bottles, and let them dangle in the lake for a while. The fish swim in."

They found a number of other children with milk bottles at the lake when they arrived there. Nobody seemed to be catching any fish though. Amy and Cynthia sat for a long time, their bottles dangling in the lake, but no fish appeared. However, something else appeared, a type of creature that every decent, well-brought-up girl by the age of ten has learned to fear and despise. These creatures are sometimes called "Pests," sometimes "Dopes," and sometimes by their most common name, "Boys." One of these boys tried to take Cynthia's bottle away from her. While he bent over, Cynthia snatched his hat from his head, cried "Salujee," and tossed the prize to Amy.

Once someone called "Salujee," and threw something to you, you had to yell "Salujee" also and pass the thing on to someone else. The whole point of the game was to make sure that the owner of the article did not get it back again. Other children joined in the game, and for a while the fish were forgotten. Somebody pushed Amy, and if Cynthia had not grabbed her in time she would have toppled into the lake. As it was, one whole leg up to her thigh became waterlogged. A glorious chase began, circling the lake, through the trees, over Indian Rock, and into the playground. Only the appearance of the park attendant and his stick put an end to the race and dispersed the armies.

Cynthia and Amy dragged homeward, with one milk bottle, a considerable amount of water and dirt on their faces and clothes, and no fish. Nevertheless, they felt it had been a fine day and that they had shown those boys a thing or two.

"You'd better change your slacks," Cynthia said, looking at Amy's bedraggled clothes. "Then we can have a game of handball in the yard."

Aunt Minnie answered the bell. Her face wore a sweet, loving smile, but only for a moment. As soon as she saw the condition of Amy's clothes, she gulped a little and then cried out, "What's the use of my killing myself washing and ironing when you just can't keep yourself clean for a minute?"

"But Aunt Minnie . . ." Amy began as she entered the house.

She never finished her sentence. Bright red and blue crepe-paper streamers decorated the living-room ceiling, and on all the walls hung red, orange, yellow, and blue balloons. From all directions, the children came running.

171

Some yelled "Happy Birthday," while others tried to give her the birthday smacks.

It really and truly was such a surprise that Amy could not say anything at all. She stood with her mouth open, looking like a perfect idiot, as Laura told her later. In the middle of the floor she saw the presents, stacked up very high it seemed.

Then Laura came toward her, smiling. "Go and wash up," she whispered, "and I'll bring you the party dress."

While Amy stood in the bathroom, washing and wondering, Laura came in, carrying her dress and shoes. Amy felt ashamed looking at Laura's happy, excited face, and she realized how much work Laura must have done to make this party for her.

"Laura . . ." she began.

"I know," giggled Laura. "You thought the party was going to be yesterday."

"Yes," answered Amy in surprise. "But how did you know?'

"Listen," smiled Laura, "you're not the smartest one in this family, even though you think you are. You wanted a surprise party, and I made sure that you had one. Wasn't it better this way — I mean, really being surprised?"

"Oh, yes," Amy said softly, feeling more and more ashamed of herself. She felt she just had to confess to Laura all about her plans for revenge.

"I'm so ashamed, Laura," she said. "I hated you so much yesterday that I was planning all kinds of mean things to get even. Are you mad at me?"

Laura just laughed. She put her arms around Amy and kissed her nose. "If you had tried anything," she said sweetly, "don't worry, I would have fixed you real good."

Amy sighed happily. She was so glad she had a sister instead of a brother. The sounds of the party came through the door, as Amy turned lovingly toward Laura and said, "You and who else?"

The Ball

When Amy knocked over her milk at breakfast that morning, Daddy jumped up from his seat and snapped at her, "For a ten-year-old, you act like a baby! It's disgraceful that a man can't have a quiet, peaceful meal in his own house."

He walked away from the table, and Amy and Laura stared after him in astonishment. It was so seldom that Daddy ever lost his temper with either one of them.

"Your father's a little upset," Aunt Minnie said gently. "Never mind, Amy, finish your breakfast or you'll be late for school." She poured Amy another glass of milk. "Of course, for a ten-year-old it is surprising how many times you do manage to knock your milk over."

Amy pushed away her cereal. "I don't want any more," she sulked.

Laura was thinking. "Why is Daddy upset?" she asked.

Aunt Minnie sat down.

"You know, Laura," she said, "your mother is getting better and better all the time, and Daddy was hoping that she would be home by summertime. Here it is the middle of May already, and she's been away nearly five months." Aunt Minnie shook her head and sighed. "But last night at the hospital the doctor told Daddy that she won't be able to come home before September. Of course," Aunt Minnie added hastily, "he also told Daddy that she is doing very well, and we should be very pleased at her recovery. They hope to take off the big cast very soon now, but it will still take a long time before Mama is strong enough to be up and around again."

Laura stood up. "I don't want any more breakfast," she said, and pushed her bowl away.

"I don't want any more either," said Amy, pushing her bowl away again. Unfortunately the bowl crashed into her glass, knocking it over and spilling the milk all over the table again.

"Nobody," Amy thought bitterly as she stood in the schoolyard waiting for the first bell to ring, "has a meaner family than mine."

First Daddy had picked on her, then Aunt Minnie, and on the way to school even Laura had told her to stop whining. "You're so selfish," Laura charged, "you never think of anybody else except yourself. Leave me alone! I feel so upset about Mama I just don't want to hear about your silly little troubles."

Amy was even angry with Mama. Why didn't Mama just tell the doctor that she wanted to go home? She could stay in bed, and the rest of them would take care of her. It wasn't as if she had pneumonia or some kind of high fever. Annette had a sick grandmother who lived with them, and her family did everything for her. Mama just didn't care.

As Amy grumbled to herself she noticed the ball lying on the ground. It seemed at first an ordinary ball, reddish-brown in color, the kind of ball the children called "spaldeens." But when Amy picked it up, she saw a picture of a cat printed on it.

"Finders keepers, losers weepers," she chanted, and held the ball in her hand as the lines of children marched up the stairs to their classrooms. After hanging up her coat, she placed the ball on her desk and examined it. The cat was rather an ordinary-looking cat, with an arched back and bristling hair. Without it, the ball would have been an ordinary ball, but with the cat it was something special.

Amy rolled the ball a little on her desk, and as she pushed it with her fingers Rosa Ferrara leaned over and whispered, "I think that is my ball."

"No, it isn't," said Amy, "it's mine."

As soon as she finished speaking, Amy wished hard that she could take it all back again. Why in the world had she lied?

"Does it have a picture of a cat on it?' Rosa continued.

"Yes."

"Well, it is my ball then. I brought it to school this morning, and I lost it."

Rosa's face wore a mild, trusting expression that infuriated Amy. She was sorry she had found the ball in the first place, but it was just like Rosa, anyway, to annoy and challenge her on a day when everything else had gone wrong too. Nobody in the class liked her or played with her, but for two terms now she and Amy had sat side by side, while Cynthia and all the interesting people sat in the back of the room. Why did she always have to get stuck?

"It's not your ball, it's mine!" she whispered angrily.

"Now what's going on over there?"

Amy looked up and found her teacher's eyes

on both of them. Her anger disappeared, and she wished the whole conversation could start over again. Rosa would say, "That is my ball," and she, Amy, would reply, "Sure, here it is." But now it was too late. She looked toward Rosa again and thought, "I can give her the ball and make up some excuse for Miss Parker." Rosa, she noticed, did not answer the teacher's question, like a tattle-tale. She just looked wonderingly at Amy.

"Perhaps I'm not speaking English," continued Miss Parker. "I said, 'What's going on over there?' "

Rosa did not reply, and with amazement Amy heard her own voice say, "She says I have her ball, but it's mine."

A sick feeling grew inside her stomach, because she knew that within a very short time Miss Parker, who knew so much, would find out the truth. Then everybody would know she was lying.

"It is my ball," Rosa said, angry now. "It has a picture of a cat on it. Nobody else has a ball like that. My aunt gave it to me."

"If it's not one thing, it's another," said Miss Parker wearily. "But if it's such an unusual ball, we won't have any trouble finding out whom it belongs to. Bring it up to my desk, Amy."

As Amy walked toward the front of the

room, she wondered if she should whisper to Miss Parker that the ball probably did belong to Rosa, but that she had a ball just like it at home. She could feel the eyes of the children upon her as she walked, and she thought desperately, "No, I can't do that. They'd know right away that I was lying."

Silently she handed Miss Parker the ball, and silently she stood by her side as the teacher looked at it. Why hadn't she stayed home from school that morning? Her throat really hurt. She must be sick, and that was why all this trouble had arisen.

"This ball has a picture of a cat stamped on it," announced Miss Parker to the class, holding it up for the children to see. "I have never seen a ball like this before. Now I'd like to know whether any of you have ever seen Rosa playing with this kind of a ball."

No hands went up.

Rosa said slowly, "This is the first time that I have brought it to school." Miss Parker nodded at her.

In a moment, Amy thought, they'll all know the truth. No one would like her anymore, and maybe even Cynthia would never speak to her again. Tears began gathering in her eyes as Miss Parker asked again. "Has anyone ever seen Amy playing with a ball like this?"

Amy heard a rustle, and saw with astonishment that just about every girl in the class had raised her hand. "But how could they?" she thought. "They never saw me playing with it." Even Annette DeLuca had her hand up in the air.

"Well, it looks as if it's your ball, Amy. I guess you made a mistake, Rosa," said Miss Parker, handing the ball to Amy.

The sick feeling in Amy's stomach disappeared. She took the ball from Miss Parker, smiled at her, and said politely, "Thank you." But how could they? she still wondered.

Rosa stood up suddenly, her face very red. "I did not make a mistake," she said. "It is my ball, and they are all liars."

Miss Parker became very angry, "You ought to be ashamed of yourself," she said. "I don't know what's happened to you today, but it's a terrible thing to be envious of what other people have, and to try to take what doesn't belong to you."

The tears began rolling down Rosa's face. Amy watched them as they came, slowly at first, and then faster and faster. "It *is* my ball," she cried. Then she said it again, but she was crying so hard that it was difficult to hear her — but Amy heard.

"Well, well," said Miss Parker in a softer voice, "there's no point in crying about it. I suppose you just made a mistake. And now we'll all forget about it and go on with our work."

As Amy walked back to her seat, Annette smiled at her and she smiled back. Bernice also smiled, and Amy noticed many of the girls looking at her and giving her friendly smiles. They really liked her, she thought happily. She wanted everybody to like her. She put the ball on the top of her desk and turned around to look at Cynthia. Cynthia winked, and she winked back.

Next to her, Rosa was crying, and Amy could hear the sounds of her sobs. "Well, it's too bad," she thought uncomfortably, "but that'll teach her a lesson, not to, not to . . ." She turned her head slowly and saw Rosa with her head down on the desk, crying so hard that her back shook. It was a strange sight to Amy, seeing Rosa cry. Many times Amy had thought that if she were Rosa she would cry. The girls still laughed at her, sometimes not even behind her back. Amy knew that often Rosa could hear the sound of their giggles as she passed. Everything she did was wrong. When 8B finally gave its spring play, Rosa's performance as the violet had been perfect. Miss Parker said proudly that she considered Rosa the star of the show. But this only served to change the resentment that most of the girls felt for Rosa into open dislike. "Poison Ivy," they whispered as she went by. She was the only girl who walked home from school alone, but she had never cried before.

Amy never joined the girls in making fun of Rosa, and whenever they said "Poison Ivy," she winced. She hated their teasing, but ever since her argument with Laura she tried not to notice it. If she interfered, maybe they would dislike her too. She just couldn't take the chance. Often she wished she could turn on the whispering, giggling girls and shout, "Stop it, you bullies, leave her alone!"

And now Rosa was crying. None of the other girls in the class, with all their teasing and giggling, had ever made her cry. But she, Amy, had done it.

She took the ball from the top of the desk and slid it inside, out of sight. Well, it was all over now, and there was nothing else she could do about it. Better to forget the whole thing. Maybe Rosa would forget also. It was too bad.

But as the afternoon passed, Amy found that she could not forget it. A number of the girls in the class spoke to her about the ball. They said Rosa was a liar and that it was just like her to try and take something that didn't belong to her.

"But did you see me playing with the ball?" Amy finally asked Helen Prendergast.

"Sure I did," said Helen. "Anyway, I think I did; and besides, I knew if you said it was yours, then it was. I certainly wouldn't believe *her*."

"It's not so much that they like me," Amy thought unhappily, "but it's more because they don't like her. Here they call her a liar, but really *they're* the liars. Why should they hate her so much? What did she ever do to them?"

After school, Amy stayed in her room and tried to read, but the memory of her lie came back to her again and again. Just look at what she had done! Not only had she involved herself in a lie, but she was responsible for all the lying hands that were raised in her defense. Every single one of them was a liar, and not a single one of them was ashamed of it. And who had suffered because of her lie? Not someone who could speak easily in her own defense, or someone who had friends to back her. Rosa had been the victim — Rosa was all alone. The memory of the small, crying figure hunched over her desk made Amy wince with shame. "What," she thought, "could be more horrible than to speak the truth, and have no one believe you because no one wanted to believe you?"

She wished she could speak to someone who could help her. Daddy and Aunt Minnie would be surprised, but somehow, she felt, they would not think it so very serious. Lying never bothered them very much. She certainly could not tell Laura, because she knew that Laura would become very angry and would feel that she had disgraced the whole family. If only Mama were home, Mama would help her. Once Mama had told her that something like this would happen, but how she wished that Mama had also told her how she might get out of it.

The ball lay on the little table in her room. She picked it up and looked at it. Imagine — a stupid, cheap little ball like that had caused all this trouble! She hated it, and she threw it hard on the floor. It felt good blaming something else, and she watched the ball as it bounded around the bedroom and finally disappeared under the bed. As soon as the ball vanished, her memories returned, and she sat thinking in the bedroom until Aunt Minnie called her to come and set the table. With a sigh, she stood up, reached under the bed, and brought the ball out again. There was only one thing to do, and she supposed she would have to do it.

The next morning Amy took the ball back to school with her. The girls seemed particularly friendly, and for a while she thought perhaps the best thing would be to forget all about it. Maybe she could just give the ball back to Rosa without anyone's seeing. She looked toward Rosa, and decided to go through with it. Her hand shot up in the air.

"Yes, Amy?" asked the teacher.

"Miss Parker," she said, "this ball belongs to Rosa." There was a rustle in the room, and Amy could hear whispers. She felt her heart beating high up in her throat as she continued. "I, I found my ball at home," She had not meant to add this last sentence, but she found herself unable to confess that she had lied. "It looks a lot like this one," she finished weakly.

"That's fine," said Miss Parker, anxious to begin work on the morning's arithmetic problems. "Give it back to her, and now suppose you all take out your notebooks."

Amy handed the ball back to Rosa, who took it without looking at her. As she sat down again in her seat, she thought, "Well, I did it, and it's all over now." But she was still not satisfied. She saw the children casually begin working on the problems, and she felt it had all happened too fast. Something still remained to be done. She raised her hand again.

"Yes," said Miss Parker pleasantly, "what is the answer?"

"Oh, it's not about the problems. It's something else."

"What is it now?" asked Miss Parker, rather sharply.

"Well, I think we should apologize to Rosa," continued Amy, hearing the rustle again. "She was telling the truth, and nobody believed her." She could feel Rosa's eyes on her face, and this time she turned away her head.

Ordinarily Miss Parker hated interruptions. She had a good deal of work planned for that morning, but as she gazed at Amy's downcast face she realized that this was no ordinary interruption.

"Yes," she said softly, "I think you are right, Amy. And Rosa, I would like to be the first to apologize." She looked around the class and continued. "I think there are others in this class who might have even better reason to apologize to Rosa. I hope they will do so, and I think they will feel much better when they do."

As Amy sat down again and looked around her, she noticed that the girls' faces did not seem as friendly as they had yesterday. Cynthia's face, in particular, disturbed her. When she turned and looked at her friend, Cynthia just frowned and shook her head. Tears rose to Amy's eyes, and she bent her head over her notebook. It was hard to lose friendships that you had worked so hard to gain, especially Cynthia's. She hoped Cynthia would not stay angry long.

But at lunchtime Cynthia did not wait for her. Amy saw her walking arm in arm with Annette, and she wondered if she should run after them. But what could she say to them when she caught up? She continued walking by herself, missing terribly Cynthia's arm to hold on to and Cynthia's ear to giggle into.

She began to wonder about Rosa, and about all the times she had walked home alone. Did she have a sister like Laura, she wondered, and why did she wear those little gold earrings? She supposed Rosa never would forgive her, but Amy was determined to wait for her after school and apologize.

That afternoon, as the lines of children marched down the stairs for dismissal, Amy kept her eyes on the long black braids ahead of her. Rosa was tiny, even smaller than Amy, but today she seemed just about the largest size girl Amy had ever seen. Out in the schoolyard, someone tapped Amy on the shoulder. She turned and found Cynthia standing behind her, not exactly friendly, but not exactly angry either.

"You sure made us look like a bunch of dopes," she said. "What's the matter with you, anyway?"

"It was the truth!" Amy said the word "truth" with such determination that even Cynthia seemed awed. "Are you mad at me?" Amy continued, softly and pleadingly.

"Well, I was," answered Cynthia, "but you're such a dope, I can't be mad at you long. Come on, let's go home."

She linked her arms through Amy's and started walking. Cynthia's arm through hers felt good, and Cynthia's friendship to Amy seemed at that point more precious than anything else.

But over there, in front of them, Rosa walked alone. She did not really seem so large now to Amy. She seemed just a small, lonely girl, walking home from school by herself.

Amy withdrew her arm slowly from Cynthia's. "I want to say something to Rosa," she said. "I'll see you later." She hurried off, without waiting for an answer. In a moment she found herself walking side by side with Rosa, and wondering desperately what to say.

"Rosa..." she began.

"I do not want to talk to you," Rosa answered, walking a little faster.

Other children from Amy's class walked on all sides of them, but for the first time Amy did not worry about them at all.

"Please don't be mad," she said. "I'm sorry."

"I told the truth, and nobody believed me," answered Rosa, "and you were lying all the time, weren't you?"

"Yes," Amy confessed sadly, "but I felt so bad yesterday when I went home that all I could do was think about it. Please don't be mad, and I promise I'll never lie again as long as I live!"

But as she spoke, the greatness of the promise struck her. Could she really go through life without ever lying, could she really?

"Well," she added weakly, "I'll try not to, anyway."

Suddenly Rosa smiled, such a sweet, forgiving smile that Amy nearly clapped her hands.

"Oh, you're not mad at me," she said, "are you? Please say you're not."

"No, not anymore," smiled Rosa.

"Can you come over to my house this afternoon and play?" bubbled Amy.

Rosa grew serious again. "I do not know," she said.

"Please come. I have a Monopoly set," Amy pleaded, "and we can play all afternoon."

"I do not know how to play Monopoly," Rosa answered shyly.

"Oh, I'll teach you. It's really very easy, and it's a lot of fun. Please come."

"I would like to," Rosa finally said, and her face grew red.

They walked on in silence for a while, and then suddenly Rosa said very shyly and softly, "You have such beautiful hair, such curls." She sighed. "I wish my hair could be like that."

"What!" cried Amy. "You think my hair is beautiful?"

She slipped her arm through Rosa's. "You know," she said confidentially to Rosa's ear, "it's a funny thing, but I always thought you had the most beautiful hair I ever saw."

Both girls giggled and continued walking arm in arm. But Amy did not tell Rosa then how long black braids tied with red ribbons had figured so often in her daydreams. She did not tell her that she thought Rapunzel's hair must have been black, and not blond at all. She would tell her later. There would be plenty of time.

Letters

June 16

Dearest Mama,

How are you feeling today? Daddy told us that they took off the big cast yesterday, and all of us are very excited. I miss you so much. Every day I keep hoping the doctors will change their minds and let you come home sooner. It's such a long time until September.

I'm sorry to have to complain in a letter to you, Mama, but I really feel you should do something about the situation here. Last night Daddy said that since you won't be home during the summer, Amy and I will have to go to camp. He said Aunt Minnie feels she needs a vacation and she wants to visit Aunt Sophie in Albany. Now that is just plain silly! First of all, why does she need a vacation? And second of all, if she does, why should she go and stay with

Aunt Sophie? After all, Aunt Sophie has three boys, and you know what boys are like!

I told her if she stays here with us she could really have a good rest. During the summer, Amy and I could get up very early in the morning, pack a lunch, and go away for the whole day. She wouldn't have to see us until suppertime. Sometimes we could even go eat at Grandma's house and sleep over. Grandma is always glad to see us. This year Aunt Rhoda and Uncle Sam aren't going away to the country until August, so we can spend a lot of time with them in July. Of course their boys are awful pests and we're mad at them right now, but I suppose we can manage to put up with them if we have to. Did I tell you what they did when we visited them last time? They filled a bag up with water and they gave it to us and said it was a present. Amy took the bag, and it began to shake, so she got scared and dropped it. Then the water ran all over the living-room rug and Aunt Rhoda came in and yelled at all of us. But it was the boys' fault. Boys are so wild!

Anyway, Aunt Minnie keeps saying she needs a vacation, even though I explain to her how peaceful it would be here. You know how stubborn she is. But even if she does go away to Aunt Sophie's, why can't I take charge of everything? After all, I'm nearly twelve and everybody says I'm very mature for my age. I've read a lot of stories about girls even younger than twelve who managed a household while their parents were away. Incidentally, did you know that Juliet wasn't even fourteen when she married Romeo?

I know how to wash clothes, and I think I can iron better than most girls my age. Do you remember, you once said that when it came to handkerchiefs I was even fussier than you? This term, I learned how to cook in school. We've only made toast, cocoa, and applesauce so far, but Miss Bennett, my cooking teacher, said the other day that if a person could read enough to read a recipe, she could cook without any trouble at all. She also said that there was a right way to cook and a wrong way.

You know, Aunt Minnie cooks applesauce the wrong way? She leaves the skins on the apples while she cooks them, and then she strains them after she's finished. But we learned in school that the right way was to peel the apples before you cook them. I explained that to Aunt Minnie, but she hates suggestions. She just asked if my teacher was married and had children. Naturally I said no, because her name is Miss Bennett. So then Aunt Minnie said she thought as much, and that the reason she peeled apples first was because she wasn't married and didn't have children. Now isn't that a silly answer?

But anyway, I'm sure I could cook. You wouldn't have to worry about Amy either, because I'd take good care of her. She's a spoiled brat, but I can manage her all right. Lately though, I think she's been improving. I like her friend Rosa Ferrara very much. She's a nice, quiet girl who is polite and respectful to older people. Not that Amy has become polite and respectful to older people, but she doesn't act as silly as she used to when she played with Cynthia all the time.

That reminds me, I have some bad news for you. Cynthia is back. For a while I thought she was really going to stay mad at Amy, and I was very glad. I felt sorry for Amy, because she went mooning around the house at first, and she went out of her way to be nice to Cynthia. But after, when

Amy got a little smarter and didn't run after her anymore, I guess Cynthia started to worry. Anyway, she came over here this afternoon with a blotter that she said she thought Amy dropped in school. Now how would she know if it was Amy's blotter? I figure she just made up an excuse to talk to Amy again. They went out to the park together, so I guess they're still friends. Too bad!

Don't forget, Mama, to talk to Daddy tonight and tell him not to send us to camp. Most of my friends will be in the city this summer, and I don't want to go away with a lot of strangers. Besides, it sounds so babyish going to camp.

I got a 96 on the history test and Dorothy Kaplan only got 95. I had the highest mark in the class, and Dorothy was very jealous. She said the only reason I get good marks is because I study, but that she gets good marks without studying. All the kids say that they don't study, but I don't think it's true. Don't be surprised if you hear that I get the highest average in the class this term. I wanted to surprise you if it happened, but I guess it just slipped out.

Well, if I write any more my hand will fall off. Don't forget to speak to Daddy tonight, and give yourself a big hug from me.

Love and x x x x x x x x x x

x x xs,

Laura

P.S. S.W.A.K. (That means "sealed with a kiss.")

P.P.S. Jeanette Farber says she went to camp once and the counselors hit the children.

P.P.P.S. Do you think I should call you and Daddy "Mother" and "Father"? Doesn't it sound more grown up?

P.P.P.P.S. I love you!!!!!!

P.P.P.P.P.S. Amy just came home. She says she will write you a real long letter tomorrow, but today she just wants to add on something to my letter. I'm going to let her, but I'll have to cover up what I wrote so she can't read it.

Dearest Mama,

How are you feeling? I am feeling fine. Tomorrow I will write you a long letter. I have some good news for you. Cynthia isn't mad at me anymore. I will tell you all about it tomorrow. I am covering this up with a blotter so Laura can't see. I don't know what she wrote you about going to camp, but I like the idea very much. She will too, once she is up there. Don't tell her what I said.

Love and x x x x x x x x x x

x x xs,

Amy

Dearest Laura,

This letter is for you. Kiss Amy, and tell her that the next letter I write will be for her. Laura darling, I know that you're not happy about going to camp, and I wish that you didn't have to go since you feel so strongly about it. But there is just no other way. The doctor won't let me come home until after the summer, and you and Amy are too young to look after yourselves. Aunt Minnie needs a vacation. I know you and Amy have done all you could to help her, and she herself has told me over and over again what sweet, good girls you both are. But you must remember, Laura, that Aunt Minnie is not used to taking care of children. She has been with you since December and needs a rest, I'm sure.

I have a feeling, though, that you'll enjoy camp very much. Just give it a chance. You're always such a good sport that I know I don't have to remind you how to behave. I worry more about Amy than I do about you. Thank goodness, you are always so dependable. Take care of your litle sister. Write soon, and have a very, very good time. I'm so happy to be able to write to you.

                              All my love,
                              Mother

                                   June 17
Dearest Mama,

How are you feeling? I am feeling fine. Laura is very cranky today. She was worse last night when Daddy came home with your letter and told us you said we should go to camp. I guess she will write you a letter today and tell you what she thinks, but don't worry, Mama, she will like it very much once she gets used to it.

I am very excited about going to camp. Last week I read a story about a girl named Susan who went to camp. The counselors were very cruel and they starved the children. So this girl Susan made all the other girls pack their clothes and march out of the camp together. Later, Susan and her friend Patricia discovered that the counselors were stealing jewels and hiding them in camp. It was very exciting.

Helen Pendergast said she went to camp last summer. She said she and her friends used to hide candy in their mattresses and used to sneak out of their bunks at night. She had a real good time.

If Aunt Minnie would not go away, I think I would rather stay in the city all summer. They built a swimming pool in the park, so I could go swimming whenever I wanted to. Rosa will be in the city during the summer, and Cynthia is only going away to the seashore for a few weeks.

I am so glad Cynthia is my friend again. She came over to the house yesterday and said she found a blotter that she thought I dropped in school. It was not mine after all, but I thanked her anyway. Then she said she guessed I was very busy lately, and I said no, I was not. Then she said she used to be my best friend, but now I did not seem to have any time for her. So I said she said she never wanted to speak to me again, but that I always wanted her to be my friend. Then she said let's make up, so we did. We went over to the park and Rosa came with us. I don't think Cynthia wanted Rosa to come with us, but she did not say anything. She showed off a lot in the park. She climbed all over Indian Rock, and when we went to the playground she hung from the top of the monkey bars by her feet. Laura says she thinks Cynthia is jealous of Rosa, but I don't think she is. Why should she be jealous? Even though I like Rosa very much, I like Cynthia too. It is silly to be jealous. After all, Cynthia likes that dope Annette, but I am not jealous.

Last week I told you that I thought I would get an A in conduct at the end of the term. But now I am not so sure. I have really tried, Mama, as you told me to. I did not pass any notes this month, and I have been sitting up so straight in my seat that my back is all stiff when I come home from school. I did not whisper much either. But yesterday I just turned around for a minute to tell Bernice Rogers, the girl behind me, to stop pushing my seat with her foot, and Miss Parker saw me. She said, "Amy Stern, I think you do more talking than any other two people in this class put together." That is not really true, Mama. Cynthia and Roslyn Brooks talk more than I do, but they sit at the back of the room and Miss Parker just does not see them. But later Miss Parker said Rosa and I could wash the blackboards for the rest of the week, so maybe she will forget what happened and give me an A in conduct. I am not counting on it though.

I think Miss Parker likes me. Yesterday, after I finished reading out loud from the reader, she said to the class, "I wish all of you could read the way Amy does." Don't you think she likes me?

I nearly forgot to tell you some more good news. I don't think Mr. Williams, the super, hates me anymore. Today after school I was feeding Buster a pretzel when Mr. Williams came up the stairs. Ever since we moved here I have been trying to get Mr. Williams to like me, so he would let me come inside the gate and play with Buster. But he never answers me when I talk to him. Today I just said, "Good afternoon, Mr. Williams," and then I was quiet. After a while he said, "You really like my dumb dog, don't you?" And I said, "Oh, yes." Then I decided to ask him, even though I thought he would chase me away. So I said, very politely, "Please Mr. Williams, could I come inside the gate sometimes and play with Buster? I will be very quiet and try not to bother you." Then he just said, "The gate's always open." I waited, but he just stood there. So I opened it very carefully and came in. We had a good time playing, Buster and I. Mr. Williams watched us for a while, then he said, "I never could figure out why you didn't come in before if you liked Buster so much." Isn't that funny, Mama? Maybe if

I asked him before he would have let me come in.

You know, Mama, when we first moved here, I did not like it as much as the old block. But now I like it better. My new friends are even nicer than my old friends. I think you will like Rosa very much when you meet her. She does not enjoy fighting either.

Daddy says you will definitely be home by September. Laura and I thought you would come home before that. Every day we used to say to each other, "Mama will probably be home tomorrow or the next day." But we never really knew. Even though September is far away, at least we know for sure now that you will be home with us then because Daddy said so. You will be surprised when you see how tall I am, and I will tell you a secret that I have not told anyone else.

I will write you another long letter tomorrow and tell you how Laura is acting.

Love and x x x x x x x x x x

x x xs,

Amy

P.S. You know, Mama, September is not really so far away, only two and a half months. Don't you think it will pass quickly? I think it will.

P.P.S. We will have good times when you come home in September. I think we always have good times when all of us are together.

P.P.P.S. Good night.